A Candlelight Ecstasy Romance

"YOU'RE JEALOUS OF MY JOB," COLBY SAID ANGRILY.

"Wrong word, buddy. Resentful. You use your job as an excuse to stay away from me," Lauren accused.

"That is not true. I like what I do and I work very hard at it because I want to make this community one that we can all take pride in. It's because of hardworking stiffs like me that the city streets are safe for you to walk on without fear of muggers, rapists, and murderers."

Lauren glared at him. "You make it sound like the whole community would fall to ruin if you weren't around to keep it in shape. You're not the only man on the police force!"

"You refuse to understand."

"Oh, I understand, all right. If I want to spend more time with you, I'll just place myself in jeopardy and holler, 'Cop!'"

CANDLELIGHT ECSTASY ROMANCES®

370 SO MUCH TO GIVE, *Sheila Paulos*
371 HAND IN HAND, *Edith Delatush*
372 NEVER LOVE A COWBOY, *Andrea St. John*
373 SUMMER STARS, *Alexis Hill Jordan*
374 GLITTERING PROMISES, *Anna Hudson*
375 TOKEN OF LOVE, *Joan Grove*
376 SOUTHERN FIRE, *Jo Calloway*
377 THE TROUBLE WITH MAGIC, *Megan Lane*
378 GOLDEN DAYS, *Kathy Clark*
379 LOVE IS ALL THAT MATTERS, *Tate McKenna*
380 FREE AND EASY, *Alison Tyler*
381 DEEP IN THE HEART, *Donna Kimel Vitek*
382 THAT SPECIAL SMILE, *Karen Whittenburg*
383 ALWAYS KEEP HIM LAUGHING, *Molly Katz*
384 A WHISPER AWAY, *Beverly Wilcox Hull*
385 ADD A DASH OF LOVE, *Barbara Andrews*
386 A STROKE OF GENIUS, *Helen Conrad*
387 THROUGH THE EYES OF LOVE, *Jo Calloway*
388 STRONGER THAN PASSION, *Emily Elliott*
389 THE CATCH OF THE SEASON, *Jackie Black*
390 MISTLETOE MAGIC, *Lynn Patrick*
391 POWER AND SEDUCTION, *Amii Lorin*
392 THE LOVE WAR, *Paula Hamilton*
393 EVENING THE SCORE, *Eleanor Woods*

LINGERING LAUGHTER

JoAnna Brandon

A CANDLELIGHT ECSTASY ROMANCE®

Published by
Dell Publishing Co., Inc.
1 Dag Hammarskjold Plaza
New York, New York 10017

ISBN: 0-440-14602-X

Printed in the United States of America

First printing—January 1986

For Maggie, with our thanks for being so patient, so understanding, so helpful.
And for our Monday-morning moms who are so very thankful to send the kiddies to school.

To Our Readers:

We have been delighted with your enthusiastic response to Candlelight Ecstasy Romances®, and we thank you for the interest you have shown in this exciting series.

In the upcoming months we will continue to present the distinctive sensuous love stories you have come to expect only from Ecstasy. We look forward to bringing you many more books from your favorite authors and also the very finest work from new authors of contemporary romantic fiction.

As always, we are striving to present the unique, absorbing love stories that you enjoy most—books that are more than ordinary romance. Your suggestions and comments are always welcome. Please write to us at the address below.

Sincerely,

The Editors
Candlelight Romances
1 Dag Hammarskjold Plaza
New York, New York 10017

CHAPTER ONE

One down and one to go, Lauren Shayler thought with a small grin of satisfaction. Her middle sister Tish had just agreed to take their grandmother for the last week of their parents' much-needed vacation, and now all she had to do was get Jeanne to take her for one of the remaining two. She felt a bit guilty asking Jeanne to help, because she already had enough on her hands with two teenaged stepchildren.

"But, dear Lord, there is no way I can take Gram for two whole weeks just now," Lauren murmured, lifting her beseeching gaze upward. All things considered, she was prepared to make any concession her sister wanted if Jeanne would agree to take Gram for the first week. The second week was hers, and she would not quibble, despite the fact that the quarter was drawing to a close and she had a mountain of paperwork to do.

"But heaven help Gram if she says *one* word about the lousy way I keep house!" Although Lauren spoke with sober emphasis, her generous mouth smiled and her large green eyes gleamed with loving indulgence. She adored her grandmother, catered to her every whim whenever possible, but nevertheless resented the fact that Catherine Shayler never visited her home without making at least one criticism, particularly about her housekeeping methods . . . or lack thereof!

"Please, please, please, don't let Donnie answer," Lauren begged a benevolent God as her neatly manicured hand reached for her personal telephone, a foot-high frog she lovingly referred to as Freddy Finklestein. The ridiculous thing was even sporting a thick toy cigar.

Donnie was Jeanne's stepson, a thirteen-year-old walking migraine if ever there was one! He had an overabundance of energy, a disgusting vocabulary, and a very big chip on his shoulder. Lauren could usually cope with him, but not on a day like today, which had started out a bummer and was getting progressively worse.

The phone rang under her hand. Startled, Lauren jerked her hand away, knocking Freddy to the floor. Glaring at the phone for having given her such a start, she retrieved it, and for a fraction of a second debated about answering, afraid it might be another of the prank calls she'd recently been receiving. Irritated by her nervousness, she was unusually short when she finally answered, identifying herself out of habit.

"Lauren Shayler, may I help you?" *If you say yes, I may scream!*

The choking sound that invaded her ear made Lauren suspect that her caller had started to laugh and checked himself. A funny little tightening sensation in her stomach told her it might be her nephew, Donnie. Annoyance puckered her brow as she muttered, "Donald Ryan Hunter, if that's you, you will never see fourteen, I can promise you that!" Her hand tightened around the phone as she indulged in a fantasy of wringing the young miscreant's neck.

Her breath caught when she heard an adult male voice say, "I think I may have the wrong number." Though it was tinged with embarrassment, the voice was one of the sexiest Lauren had ever heard, the sort of throaty drawl that can start a romantic-at-heart dreaming of warm, balmy nights, of dancing barefoot in the dark, of lying on a moonlit beach sipping Margaritas . . . all with just the right man.

As owner/operator of the Speedy Answering Service, Lauren had heard various types of voices. There had been times when she'd correctly matched a voice to its owner, and then there had been times when she'd been grossly wrong. This man sounded absolutely scrumptious. Tall, blond, and handsome with just the right amount of brawn and plenty of sex appeal, if the voice was anything to go by.

Lauren relaxed her grip on the phone. "Oh, don't let that upset you," she murmured consolingly. She smiled with relief. *At least you're not Donnie,* she thought thankfully. "I've answered more wrong numbers today than you could shake a stick at."

"The unflappable type, aren't you?" the man teased. The laughter that followed was rich, full-bodied, and it swirled inside her ear, delighting her with the amusement he was making no great effort to disguise.

"I try to be." A glance at the digital clock on her desk reminded Lauren that unless she made her call to Jeanne within the next ten minutes, she would have to wait until after dinner to call. And she was impatient to get everything arranged immediately.

Trying not to sound unfriendly, she said, "I hope the next time you dial, you'll be a little more careful and get the number you want." Without waiting for his response, Lauren depressed the disconnect button. After a bit she withdrew her finger, lifted the phone to her ear, and discovered that the connection had not been broken.

An irrational anger came over her with little warning. Lauren had to fight to keep it from showing in her voice. "Uh, if you don't mind, would you hang up so I can make a call?" She hung up and then sat back, mentally counting to thirty before reaching for the phone again.

Rats! she thought when the phone rang under her hand again. She lifted it and managed somehow to keep her cool as she said, "Hello?"

To her disgust the only sound she heard was heavy breathing.

"Oh, fudge!" This had to be her lucky day, she thought

sarcastically. A wrong number and now the heavy breather who had been plaguing her for the past week or so.

"Look, you miserable creep, enough's enough!" Her voice was tight with irritation, her expression murderous. "Get off my line and stay off! If you persist in harassing me, I am going to turn the matter over to the police. And I guarantee you, you will not like their methods!" Trembling with anger and frustration, she dropped the phone.

Lauren's eyes looked like a storm-swept sea as she stood a few seconds later looking out the window that faced the street. Her back was rigid, and her small chin was thrust out in a very characteristic manner, the Don't-tread-on-me! warning that everyone who knew her understood all too well. Her fingers tapped angrily on the windowsill while her mind whirled with chaotic thoughts.

The world outside was slowly growing darker, and the wind had come up. Orange, red, and yellow leaves were falling from the maple trees in her front yard, creating a colorful blanket across the kidney-shaped lawn. The tree roses that bordered the lawn had long ago lost their blossoms, but a camellia stuck under the eaves had obviously lost track of the seasons and was sporting a lovely pink-streaked white bloom which the wind was doing its best to destroy.

Lauren pressed her forehead to the windowpane and closed her eyes, taking pleasure in the coldness of the glass. Long, wispy tendrils of pale blond hair that had escaped the confines of her French roll fell forward, lightly brushing her high cheekbones, tickling the tip of her small, straight nose. But Lauren didn't notice. She was too busy trying to make sense of what had been happening lately.

Was the miserable man changing his modus operandi? Normally, he called at night. She knew she should report the nuisance caller to the phone company or the police, and she would. But first, she had to call Jeanne. Lauren turned away from the window and went to her desk.

Her elder sister Jeanne was a creature of habit. Every afternoon at five she went jogging. But maybe today she was off schedule. Lauren shrugged. It was worth a try.

A pensive cloud darkened her eyes to deep emerald. Jeanne was not so much interested in jogging as she was in socializing with her neighbors, particularly the children. She had a fervent hope that through them she would learn more about what made her own stepchildren tick.

"Poor Jeanne." Lauren admired her older sister, but more often than not, that admiration was glossed with pity. Jeanne was fighting a losing battle. A weaker woman might have thrown in the towel long ago, but Jeanne was passionately dedicated to getting her two stepchildren back on the right track. She insisted that Donnie and sixteen-year-old Jill were just confused, that what they desperately needed was a lot of understanding liberally honeyed with tender loving care, which she was prepared and more than willing to supply if only the children would allow her.

The phone rang, derailing Lauren's train of thought. She frowned at it, suspecting it was the heavy breather again. Should she answer it and once more give him the satisfaction of annoying her? she wondered as she lowered herself into her desk chair.

"Damn!" She had wanted to be strong, to drive the jerk straight up the proverbial wall by ignoring him, but her curiosity won out and she hurriedly reached for the receiver.

Her mouth opened to issue a caustic reprimand, but the brilliant words she had chosen died somewhere between her brain and voice box.

"Anne, darling?" whispered the sexy male voice that had impressed her a little while ago.

Distracted by the sensual appeal of the man's voice, Lauren lost her opportunity to tell him that he had once again dialed the wrong number.

"Listen, darling," he continued, "I'm really very sorry that I'm so late in calling you." He laughed, the warm husky tones sending a little shiver of delight tingling up Lauren's spine.

"I did try to call by a quarter to five like you wanted, but I kept getting some dizzy broad who claims she's spent her entire day answering wrong numbers." He laughed heartily. "She's probably an old maid lonesome for company who gets her jollies that way." He laughed again, but this time the sound was soft and seductive. By now, Lauren was heartily sick of him and reacted with an indelicate snort.

The man hesitated and then, perhaps in an effort to tease a laugh out of his 'darling Anne,' he added, "She probably even answers pay phones too."

Lauren's chin went up a notch and her eyes flashed mutinously. Family and friends knew these were storm warnings, but, of course, the man on the other end of the line had not the slightest inkling that one was about to break over his impudent head.

"This is not 'Anne, darling,'" Lauren mimicked frigidly. "This is the 'dizzy broad' with the phone fetish." Her breath was coming in short, ragged gasps. "Now, hang up, pea brain, and try again. Maybe 'darling Anne' will find you amusing. I sure as hell don't!" It would have pleased her immensely to slam down the receiver, but curiosity stayed her hand, and she waited for his reaction, entertaining a vague hope that he would stumble over an apology that she had every intention of throwing back in his ear.

"Kook!" he said. Mocking laughter lingered in the wake of his swift disconnect.

"Look who's calling whom a kook!" Lauren slammed down the receiver. "Turkey!" She was furious with the man for having insulted her, and angry with herself because she had allowed his voice to captivate her.

Jeanne would be gone by now. But Lauren was so out of sorts, she dialed the number of the Hunter residence anyway. She felt a childish need to brawl with someone. And, of

16

course, she knew Donnie was always ready, and eager, to oblige.

"Hello!" a friendly male voice greeted.

Rob. The wind went out of Lauren's sails. She liked her brother-in-law.

"Hi, Rob. This is Lauren." She managed to sound cheery.

"Oh, hi, Laurie. What can I do for you?"

"You can have Jeanne call me when she's through amusing the neighborhood with her version of the Olympic sprint," she teased, and Rob laughed. "Tell her she can call me up to eleven o'clock, please."

"Will do."

"Thanks, Rob. I'll return the favor sometime."

"How about next week?" There was a strained quality to his voice that made Lauren stiffen involuntarily.

"Is something wrong, Rob?"

"Nothing Jeanne and I can't handle, with a little bit of help from the rest of the family."

Oh, no! was all Lauren had time to think before Rob plunged ahead.

"Jeanne and I have appointments with all of Donnie's teachers and most of Jill's next week. My mind would rest a lot easier if I knew the kids were with you while we're doing that. Can you pick them up from school every day and take them back to your place?"

"I . . ." Lauren sighed. Five years ago, when Jeanne had announced she was marrying the widowed Councilman Hunter, the entire Shayler family had vowed to help whenever and wherever they were needed. Recalling that she had been as vehement as her mother on this, Lauren acquiesced.

"Thank you, Laurie," Rob said, and she sensed relief in his voice.

"My pleasure," she lied, then said good-bye.

Lauren felt vaguely tearful as she lowered her head to her crossed arms on the desk blotter. She closed her eyes against a faint throbbing in her temples. If Jeanne was going to be

17

busy with teacher conferences all week . . . Lauren sighed dispiritedly. She would simply have to rearrange her own schedule, and let Gram stay with her next week.

Yet that was not what had her suddenly feeling that the world at large was out to get her. To say that she was not looking forward to the following week was a gross understatement. She could handle Donnie by himself for brief periods of time, and she could cope with Jill if she ignored the teenager's "snotty" attitude, but having to put up with the two of them together? And on the same week that Gram would be staying with her? Lauren groaned.

"Oh, well," she whispered a moment later. She would not let the "Katzenjammer Kids" get to her. She stood, tucked flyaway strands of hair behind her ears, and then headed toward the kitchen for a snack. One of the best fringe benefits of being self-employed and running the business from her home was that she could raid the refrigerator as frequently as she wanted during the day.

She had just opened the refrigerator when she heard one of the business lines ringing. Lauren frowned. It was Friday and all the businesses she serviced closed at five. But since they were her bread and butter, she decided to forsake her quest for food in favor of answering the phone.

"Warm and Free, Limited," she literally sang into the speaker. "May I help—?" Her voice froze, and her eyes rounded with shock when a male voice cut in abruptly with some rather explicit sexual suggestions.

The thing to do in this sort of situation, Lauren knew, was to hang up. She had done that on other occasions, but this time her wits were so scattered she could not gather them long enough to cut the scum off. So she sat there, unable to move or speak, an unwilling audience for a male whose vulgarities seemed endless.

Sensibilities totally scandalized, Lauren finally broke the connection. She stayed where she was, trembling, her face blanched, her eyes wide with mortification, slow tears rolling unnoticed down her cheeks.

Stumbling over the most wicked imprecation she knew did not ease the impotent anger surging through her. At the moment the only thing that might have given her any satisfaction was to see the vile creature being pulled in four different directions by galloping horses.

Until now, she had considered her business lines sacrosanct. Her turbulent green gaze swept across the old-fashioned switchboard panel. Thirty-six lines. She whimpered, knowing that the slime must be caught soon; he would have a field day if he gained access to all of them.

Too upset to follow normal procedure, Lauren didn't waste time by reporting the calls to the telephone company. She dialed the police.

When the desk sergeant who answered her call grumbled that their office had recently been deluged with similar reports, Lauren decided she was about to get the fast shuffle. She felt her temper rise. She wasn't without compassion, but while she sympathized with all the other victims, she felt more vulnerable than they. Her situation was different, more severe. She operated a telephone answering service and deserved special, immediate attention.

Still, Lauren realized nothing would be gained by antagonizing the police officer. She took a deep breath. "I am not normally this difficult to get along with, Sergeant," she explained, her voice thankfully calm. "However, I run a phone answering service from my home. Together with my personal line it gives this—this scuzzball thirty-seven phones to play his smutty games on, with me as his sole victim." Her voice cracked, and she had to bite down on her lower lip to keep herself from bursting into tears.

The ensuing silence was strained, and Lauren wondered if the officer was still on the line. And then, in a voice that told her he was forcing himself to remain patient, he said that someone would look into her problem. Lauren had to be satisfied with that, so she thanked him politely and hung up.

She didn't know how long it would take for that "someone" to get back to her, so she decided to stay busy until he did. During the past six months she had picked up five additional accounts, which meant that she had to work on her books every single day if she wished to stay current. She pulled out her ledgers and went to work, determined to keep her misery at bay.

"A body could be drawn and quartered and put on picks for public viewing before the police showed up," she grumbled as she put the ledgers away. Almost two hours had passed since she'd called them, and thus far she had only the desk sergeant's word that someone would follow up on her complaint.

She glanced at the phone, wondering if she ought to call again, when she heard a knock on her door.

Lauren rose and moved toward the door. Then she stopped. Supposing the smut-mouth had come to make good on his kinky promises? *No!* She shook her head violently, then started backing away, eyes dark with apprehension focused on the closed door.

The knock was repeated, so loud and imperious that it seemed to reverberate through the room. Lauren blinked herself into alertness and again began moving to the front door, one hesitant step at a time. She had no idea who was standing on her porch, but she hoped with all her heart that it was not her tormentor. Her hand trembled as she reached out, touched the doorknob, then recoiled. Her eyes scanned upward, and she assured herself that the deadbolt was secure. She relaxed, but only slightly.

"Who's there?" She spoke in a faint echo of her normally low and husky voice.

"Police, Miss . . . Shayler. May I come in and talk to you?"

Finally! Relief flooded through her. Eager fingers fumbled

20

with the deadbolt, undid it, reached for the doorknob, curled around it, and froze. Anyone could claim to be the police merely to gain entrance to her home.

Her lips curled with a derisive grin. *My momma didn't raise no fool here, mister!* she thought, managing to shore up her sagging courage.

"How can I be certain you are who you say you are?" she demanded.

"I could show you my badge," the voice offered helpfully.

For that she would, of course, have to open the door. *No way, José!*

"Send it through the transom," she instructed. She stepped back to wait, lifting an expectant gaze to the window her father had installed over the front door. "Along with your identification, if you please," she added hastily, but no less firmly.

Amused laughter drifted through the door. Lauren frowned pensively. There was something vaguely familiar about that laugh. . . .

"Here goes," the man said cheerfully, "but you make sure you return them, all right?" In a flash he had sent the requested items to her through the transom. Lauren was not swift enough to catch them in midair; they dropped to the floor by her feet.

"Satisfied?" he asked a moment later.

"Not quite," she snapped. "First tell me your sergeant's name."

"Hanson. Gordon Hanson."

"You won't mind, then, if I call him to make sure you are who you say you are?"

"Not at all" was the curt rejoinder. "Take all the time you want, Miss Shayler. I do my best investigating on front porches."

His sarcasm bordered on hostility, but Lauren ignored it and hurried to the phone. Quickly dialing the number she'd dialed earlier, she asked to speak to Sergeant Gordon Hanson.

"Speaking. How can I help you?"

"Is, ah . . ." She flipped open the brown-leather case, and scanned the information on the identification card. "Colby Sherman. Is he in?"

"Uh, no, he's not, miss. If it's, uh, personal, you can try him in the morning. He's usually in by eight. If not, maybe I can help you?"

"As a matter of fact, you can." She felt and sounded breathless, and her heart seemed to be doing the jitterbug in the middle of her throat. "Describe him to me, please."

There was a long, tense moment of silence, and then Gordon Hanson laughed. "I don't know that I can, miss. The lieutenant's—"

"Describe him as though you were describing a wanted man," Lauren interrupted tersely. Gordon Hanson heaved a great sigh, then started ticking off the information she wanted. Lauren checked it against the ID card in her hand and concluded that she owed Colby Sherman an apology.

"Thank you," she remembered to say before she put down the receiver. Hesitantly, she approached the door.

"Now are you satisfied?" the man claiming to be Colby Sherman demanded impatiently.

Lauren frowned. She had not liked his tone. "Not quite," she responded. "Tell me your height, weight, color of hair and eyes."

"I don't know why you were so frightened of an obscene caller," was his disgruntled response. "You could have questioned him to death!"

"Maybe that's what I'm doing!"

The man muttered something Lauren could not make out, and then complied. "Let me see, now. Height, six three. Weight, one eighty-eight. Hair, blond. Eyes, hazel." With a short, gruff laugh he added, "In case you're interested, I was born August ninth, nineteen fifty. I don't bite"—he paused

22

as the door started to open. A sprite whose slightly disheveled head barely reached to his chest and whose eyes rivaled the beauty of an emerald came into view—*"much!"*

So this is Lauren Shayler! And to think that I came expecting to find a spinster who sees a pervert behind every bush, he thought, his eyes brightening with appreciation as they conducted a swift but thorough inspection of the woman he'd spoken to earlier in the day when he'd twice dialed the wrong number.

She was petite and looked soft and delicate in a short gray skirt and pink-and-gray striped blouson. She was barefoot. Colby's mouth twitched as his gaze lingered on her toes. Her nails were painted a hot pink and were decorated with decals of unicorns and exotic birds.

At last her posture penetrated his concentration. Lauren was braced with one hand on the wall and the other on the door. A curious frown puckered Colby's forehead. Was she planning to keep him out on the porch while they talked? Or could it be she intended to slam the door in his face if he didn't meet with her approval? His mouth curved with a faint smile.

Lauren had intended to berate him for taking so long to get to her, but her brain seemed to have softened to mush as she stood there staring at him. Colby Sherman was a hunk from the top of his tawny head to the tips of his shiny black boots.

He had a face that belonged on the covers of the ever-popular books of romantic fiction. His nose was straight, narrow; his mouth was sensually curved, generous but not too full. The cheekbones were well defined, high; the cheeks contoured down to a strong, firm chin. At the moment there was an arrogant tilt to his squarish jaw which gave him a rugged, somewhat intimidating look.

Here was a man who probably played as hard as he worked, Lauren decided, unashamedly treating herself to a second appraisal of Colby Sherman. There wasn't an ounce

of fat evident through the pale-blue shirt that snugly outlined the length of his torso, and she would make book on
her guess that the long legs encased in dark-blue slacks were
sinewy and strong.

Belatedly recalling why the man was there, Lauren
glanced up and found him smiling. The quality of that smile
told her he was aware of her scrutiny and was amused by it.

"You don't even look like a cop," she blurted.

He smiled. "I usually don't. Besides, I work plainclothes."

Lauren nodded and said, "Come in, won't you?" She
stepped aside to allow him entry into her home. As he went
past her, she held out his badge and card case.

"Thank you," Colby said, smiling. "There's no telling
when I'll be needing them again." Despite the mocking tone
his drawling voice had a vague familiarity about it, but
Lauren dismissed it as the workings of an overactive imagination.

Moving her hands behind her, she placed them flat against
the closed door and studied Colby as he began to prowl
around her living room–office. He had a very sensual walk,
one that did very strange things to her pulse rate.

It was too bad that the only attractive male under forty
who had crossed her threshold in over three months was
there only in an official capacity, Lauren thought ruefully.
Sighing, she pushed away from the door and crossed the
gold-carpeted room to her desk.

CHAPTER TWO

Windows left ajar, drapes wide open so just *anyone* could see into the room. . . . Colby shook his head, despairing of women who lived alone and made victims of themselves in this very manner.

Taking a notebook and pen from his shirt pocket, he made a quick note: *Lives alone.* And then he turned slowly to look at Lauren.

"Is there something wrong with this window, Miss Shayler?" he asked, watching her expression as he spoke, almost positive she would look surprised to discover that the window was broken. "It won't close all the way."

Lauren blinked. What correlation a broken window had with a wacko who got his jollies from annoying her on the phone, she couldn't even imagine. But as the lieutenant seemed to be waiting for an answer, she supplied it, albeit grudgingly. "It's broken. Daddy's my handyman and he—"

The surprised quality of his "Oh?" combined with the swift ascent of one tawny eyebrow made Lauren bristle. Her chin went up. "He's been busy with other projects," she stated rather crisply.

"Take it easy, Miss Shayler," Colby said, his voice husky with amusement. "There's no need to get defensive with me."

Ha! that's what you think! The way he was looking at her was enough to start a whole butterfly farm in her stomach.

Lauren took a hasty step backward as Colby stepped closer to her.

"I'm sorry," she mumbled. "I wasn't aware that I sounded defensive."

Liar! his quick smile seemed to taunt.

Lauren forced a smile and went on, desperately trying to keep her voice cool and unemotional. "The fact is that my father *has* been rather busy lately." So busy, in fact, that his physician had had to resort to scare tactics to convince him he needed a rest.

Hmmm. Colby's mouth quirked a little as he glanced down and made another notation. Obviously no steady fellow in her life . . . for now.

"Have it fixed as soon as possible," he said, nodding toward the window. "It's unwise to allow things like that to go uncorrected."

A vague frown lined Lauren's brow. She felt as if he were passing judgment on her father, finding fault with *him.* Her annoyance with Colby was blatantly revealed in the tautness of her expression as she suggested, "Shall we get on with what you're really here for, Lieutenant?"

If looks could kill, the heat of Colby Sherman's prolonged stare should have burned her to a crisp. His hazel eyes narrowed, hardened, and the mouth Lauren had found so sensually attractive mere seconds before thinned with a grim smile. But Lauren didn't care. Cop or not, he had no right to criticize her father, even by implication.

"Shall we get started, then, Miss Shayler?"

"Let's do," she whispered to his strong back as Colby moved toward the chair by the switchboard.

Propping the pad on his knee, Colby poised the pen over it and mentally geared himself to go through the motions of a full-fledged investigation. But only because he knew this was what Lauren expected. He had a hunch that the "nuisance calls" she had reported were the ones he'd made to her number by mistake.

Self-derision darkened the hue of his irises and put a crooked smile on his mouth. He should've assigned someone from the night shift to follow up on her complaint, because now that he had seen Lauren Shayler, he had a burning, totally irrational desire to know her.

Catching his smile, Lauren felt equal parts of annoyance and appreciation.

And more than a little impatience.

"In the interest of saving time, Lieutenant, why don't I just tell you what's been happening, and if you have any questions, you can ask them later, all right?" Her voice was deliberately conciliatory.

Colby gave her a swift, ominous look and clenched his back teeth. Damn! How can she look so sweetly delicate and be so pushy!

"Be my guest," he invited curtly.

He sounded angry. One quick look at his face made her realize that he was displeased with her. But why? And then it hit her. The Lieutenant had obviously had his Joe Friday routine ready to spring on her, and in her haste to unburden her problem, she had deprived him of the chance.

Sorry, she thought, shrugging off his annoyance. After all, she had more to worry about than whether Colby Sherman was or wasn't happy with her.

"The calls started coming last week—"

"As far back as that?" He took a swift, silent breath of relief, and studied her thoughtfully as he waited for her to continue.

"Ten days ago, to be precise."

He nodded, shifted his weight on the chair, then leaned back to ease the tension from his lower back. "Go on, Miss Shayler," he prompted, his gaze intent on her face. His voice was cool and businesslike; his features were a perfect mask of sobriety.

"Like I said, the first of many calls came ten days ago. And with each subsequent call the jerk got a little bolder,

27

and a lot more graphic with his smutty talk." She took a swift, noisy breath. "Today was the last straw. He said that—" Abruptly she stopped, and her cheeks flushed crimson with embarrassment. She couldn't do it. She had thought she could, but here she was, unable to give even the tiniest hint as to what the sleaze had said to her. It was ridiculous, she knew, but even now she could hear the voice whispering across her memory, and it made her feel crawly all over. She started to shudder, caught herself. She closed her eyes briefly, in a moderately successful attempt to restore her composure.

Colby had stopped writing when she stopped talking. In watchful silence he took in the fading blush on her cheeks, the quivering of her lower lip, the hurt and rage that darkened her eyes. In the brief time that he had been with her, he had witnessed various emotions flitting over those beautiful features, but until now, vulnerability had not been one of them.

Suddenly anger welled inside him and he wanted to hit the vermin who had frightened her. It was all he could do to keep his voice level as he prompted, "What was so different about today?"

He waited a moment, and when she didn't answer, he repeated, "What was so different about today, Lauren?" He hated to press, to force her to remember what was doubtlessly too painful, too humiliating, for her, but he needed to know. "What was it he said? Did he threaten you in some way?"

"He said . . ." Whether it was the disquieting, intent manner in which this man was studying her or the memory of that miserable call that was making her feel breathless, Lauren couldn't decide. She breathed deeply and then forced herself to continue. "He told me . . . filth . . . garbage . . . like the graffiti scratched on public-bathroom walls." She closed her eyes, partly to avoid Colby's avid gaze, and partly to chase away the memory of that evil man.

For a moment Colby gazed out the window, distractedly taking pleasure in the sunset that washed the western sky in varied hues of gold, orange, and red. When he felt that Lauren was composed enough to listen to what he had to say, he turned to face her.

"There are several ways to discourage this kind of harassment," he began, giving her a brief smile. "By far the easiest is to change your number."

A smile faintly curved Lauren's mouth, but there was no warmth, no sign of amusement, in the eyes that focused unblinkingly on his face. "I run an answering service, Lieutenant," she explained, sounding as though she were delivering a well-rehearsed speech. "There are thirty-six businesses who depend on me to keep them in touch with their customers. I cannot see myself asking even one of them to change his number simply because . . ." She shrugged and cast her eyes downward, to the hands she had unconsciously clasped on her lap.

In his mind Colby filled in the rest. ". . . the police can't be bothered to find the creep with the phone fetish." He tightened his jaw, mentally counted to ten, and then said, "I was under the impression that the calls were made to your personal line."

"Until today they were." Lauren flashed a glance at the switchboard, and her eyes sparked with anger and frustration as she turned to look at him again. "If this call hadn't come in on a business line, I would not have bothered you."

Independent little cuss, aren't you? Colby thought, secretly amused.

"I'm glad you did, Miss Shayler. That's what we're here for." He shifted uncomfortably, strangely unnerved by the way she was looking at him. Dammit! He wasn't the one harassing her. Why the devil did she have to look so bloody unfriendly? Again he shifted uneasily.

If he was trying to make himself comfortable, he was wasting his time, Lauren thought. The chair was not built to

29

hold someone his size. It was strictly utilitarian, chosen specifically to discourage her from getting too sedentary.

"That chair by the window is much more comfortable. Why don't you sit over there?" she suggested, directing Colby's attention to the big overstuffed chair in front of the broken window.

A weary smile played over his expressive features as Colby cast a longing glance at the chair. It was covered in rich brown leather, and it looked extremely cozy, particularly with the matching ottoman positioned at just the right distance to accommodate someone with very long legs. Daddy? he wondered. Or had he made a mistake thinking this sexy kitten was momentarily without a male friend? And why in blazes did the thought of her having a steady fellow annoy him?

Irritated by the direction in which his thoughts were roving, Colby shook his head. "I don't think so." He rose abruptly, snapped his notebook closed, and returned it to his shirt pocket. "I believe I have all I need."

Lauren resisted the urge to say, *Bully for you, but what about me?* Instead, she asked quietly, "What happens now, Lieutenant?"

"I'd advise you to change the number on your personal phone immediately, and keep the new number unlisted. The call to your business line was probably just an isolated incident," he said. "I don't think it'll be repeated."

For an instant Lauren looked aghast. Dammit! He was sweeping her problem under the rug! Her eyes sparkled with rising anger. Then her expression changed as she thought that blowing her cool would gain her nothing. "But what if it is?" she asked, somehow managing to keep her exasperation with him from showing in her voice. "What if today's call was just the beginning? In case I neglected to point it out before, there are a total of thirty-six business lines in this house."

Colby lost his opportunity to answer, because by now

Lauren had gathered a head of steam and railed at him, "There's no telling how many of the numbers that miserable scuzzball has. What if he has all of them and decides to terrorize me at his whim? What do I do then, Lieutenant?" she demanded, lifting a challenging look to his face.

His voice was a lot cooler than his temper as Colby explained, "If the calls should start again, I want you to keep track of the exact time each call comes in and then report in to me . . . or to Gordon Hanson. I'll brief him about you." He forced a smile. "And—"

"And then what?"

Damn! Colby clenched his jaw for control. The woman had an annoying habit of interrupting. He mentally counted to ten and managed a tight smile. "Then we can trace your breather through the telephone company and—"

"He's not my breather, thank you!"

Her huffy reaction amused him, distracted him from his anger. Colby chuckled.

"I'm delighted you find my situation so amusing, Lieutenant." The very softness of her voice shamed him.

"I apologize for laughing," he said, hastily sobering his expression, although laughter echoed in his voice as he added, "I guess I didn't think how that would sound."

He wasn't the least bit repentant, and they both knew it. Lauren fumed as she hurried across the room to open the door. As far as she was concerned, this interview was over.

As she waited, somehow managing not to show her impatience by tapping her foot, she contemplated her options and concluded that it was, and probably always had been, up to her to get rid of the caller. The lieutenant, for some ungodly reason she could not fathom, insisted on creating a molehill out of what, to her, seemed an unscalable mountain.

Colby didn't need to see the open door to know that Lauren was annoyed with him. And though he himself couldn't comprehend his reasons, he felt a need to leave

Lauren with a good impression. He went to her, determined to make her smile.

"Will you be all right?" His voice was a soft whisper of concern, but his eyes studied Lauren's set features with an intensity that was destined to add to her displeasure with him.

Icicles clung to her voice as she retorted, "I suppose I'll have to be."

It angered him that she should be so damned unfriendly. Tight jawed, clinging to his control with both hands, Colby stressed, "That window needs to be fixed, pronto, Miss Shayler." He pointed to the security risk with his pen before slipping it into his shirt pocket. "And I would suggest you don't wait to get your number changed." He stared down at her and came up against the power of beguiling green eyes and a mouth that looked warm and inviting, if somewhat petulant.

Colby took a deep breath and drew in the clean, almondy smell of her hair. He said, or thought he did, "You'll be all right once you get a new number." His gaze was fixed on her mouth, a mouth he wanted desperately to taste. He shook his head and unconsciously pulled himself up to his full height, struggling against an overwhelming, confusing, and totally illogical desire to take her in his arms.

Fate, in the form of the ringing phone, intervened, drawing Lauren's attention away from Colby and giving him the perfect excuse to delay leaving her. He saw the apprehensive look that clouded her eyes, took in the stiffening of her slight shoulders, and realized that she was genuinely frightened. Her plight touched a tenderness in him he could not remember having felt for any other woman, and called forth his male instinct to protect.

"Let me get that for you," he said, starting toward the phone. Lauren stopped him with a hand on his arm.

"That would be so easy," she admitted, smiling shakily.

32

"But, thank you, no. I have to do this myself. If you don't mind, though, I'd like you to stay."

"Of course." Colby smiled as he went to the chair by the window. With a grateful, somewhat weary sigh, he lowered himself into it.

Drawing courage from his presence, Lauren walked to the phone and picked it up. "Hello?" she said confidently, secretly praying her courage would hold.

"Hello, Sis." It was Jeanne's serene voice, not the gritty, insulting voice she had expected. Lauren nearly collapsed with relief.

Holding the phone to her breast, she turned to Colby and mouthed the words "My sister," and then sat down to talk to Jeanne.

Colby had been raised with two female cousins and knew from long experience that when sisters got on the phone, they usually gossiped. Noticing the lounging position Lauren had assumed at her desk, he decided this was going to be a long siege, and he might as well relax.

He stretched out his long legs, resting his feet on the ottoman, and gave himself over to studying his surroundings.

The room was enormous, done in bright, sunny colors that made it warm, homey. It was obvious that whoever had decorated the room went in for antiques, as evidenced by the immense rolltop desk at which Lauren sat, a tall hutch in the corner, an armoire set flush against the same wall as the dark-blond, L-shaped wooden table that contained the switchboard panel, an electric typewriter, and a small television set.

His gaze lazily swept over the rest of the furnishings, and finally came to rest on the massive tan-leather couch in front of the huge fireplace.

A whimsical smile spread over Colby's features. With nothing better to occupy his mind, he indulged an erotic fantasy. He pictured a low fire in the fireplace, lightly crackling, throwing a faint glow over the two healthy, tanned bodies that were entwined on the buttercup-yellow hearth-rug. Two glasses and a bottle of vintage wine were temporarily forgotten as the two sated other thirsts.

A blast of amused laughter shattered his daydream, and Colby's eyes opened wide to stare at Lauren.

". . . and the only diversion I've had all day was when this joker got me by mistake while he was trying to call his girl." Her warm laughter rang out again, echoing with mockery. "You should've heard him! The macho man was in such a sweat to apologize to his 'darling Anne,' he kept misdialing and getting me." She giggled. "I can't recall ever hearing a male in such a panic!" Recalling how insulting the man had been, she sobered, her forehead puckering with a frown.

"He did have a very sexy voice, though," she added musingly.

What was that old saying about eavesdroppers never hearing the best about themselves? Colby could not decide whether her appreciation of his "sexy voice" was any consolation in view of what she'd said about his aborted calls to Anne.

Anne!

His eyes narrowed with irritation when he remembered the ultimatum she'd handed him when he finally got through to her. "Be on time tonight, Colby, or don't bother calling me again," she'd said. A swift glance at his wristwatch showed that he was already more than an hour late for their date.

He leaned his head back again and closed his eyes with a disgruntled sigh. He'd known for a while that there was no future in their relationship, but he hadn't wanted things to end on such a bitter note!

The sound of soft footfalls approaching brought his dismal thoughts to an abrupt halt. Colby's eyes fluttered open, glanced up, brightened, as they appraised the lovely creature walking toward him. Smiling with appreciation, he straightened, slowly dropping his feet from the ottoman.

Lauren liked his smile, responded to it with a warm, crooked grin. As she came to a stop tantalizingly close to him, she saw that his hair was mussed and wondered what thoughts had made him rake his fingers through it. A stubborn curl lay across his brow, like a swath of gold silk. She wanted to touch it, to smooth it back with her fingers and ease away the fatigue that lined his forehead. Instead, she folded her arms across her midriff.

"I'm sorry I took so long." She smiled. "I had to discuss something with Jeanne, and if I didn't do it today, it would have plagued me all night."

"We wouldn't want that," he said, rising in one surprisingly fluid movement. He stood so close to her, Lauren could feel his breath fanning the wispy tendrils of hair that lay across her forehead. She forgot to breathe, and her knees suddenly seemed to have all the substance of a limp dishrag.

Time seemed arrested. Lauren looked up at Colby, her eyes big, round with expectancy. She was taking very small, shallow breaths, unwilling to disturb the mood.

Colby allowed himself the dangerous luxury of gazing into her emerald eyes. He felt drawn to their depths, and instinctively, he started to bend down toward the softness of the mouth that looked so moist and inviting. The seductive flavor of her perfume drifted into his nostrils, caressed his senses, made his body tingle with desire.

Her breath came out in a ragged sigh, breaking the spell. Abruptly, she became aware that she was straining toward him, taxing the tips of her toes, practically throwing herself at the man. Hastily, she composed herself and stepped back and away, leaving Colby holding empty air, all that remained behind when his hands had reached out to hold her.

He made a nervous movement with his neck and shoulders. "Since you appear to be all right, I guess I'll be going now." His voice was huskier than normal even to him, and in an attempt to regain a semblance of normality, he reiterated, "Get the window fixed, and call the phone company tomorrow about changing your number."

Lauren nodded. As she went to the door, she murmured, "I will on Monday, just as soon as—" Then the phone rang. She halted in midstep. A feeling of inevitability washed over her and she stood staring over her shoulder at poor Freddy as though the frog had suddenly come to life. She trembled inwardly, unable to take a step in any direction.

When Colby touched her shoulder, she nearly jumped out of her skin. The look she gave him was full of horror.

"Would you like me to get that for you?" he whispered.

"I have to get it myself," she mumbled, but made no move toward the phone.

Long, virile fingers slid around her elbow with unbelievable gentleness and slowly, very slowly, Colby urged Lauren to move with him. It was his hand that picked up the receiver, his hand that held it to her ear, and his cheek that pressed against hers to listen with her.

Dimly, Lauren's mind registered the slight roughness of whiskers on his cheek, the warmth of his skin, and the subtle mingling of spicy cologne and his own male scent.

"He—hello?" Nervous anticipation constricted her throat, prickled the skin at the back of her neck, and made her voice hoarse.

A raspy male voice mocked, "Dear, dear Laurie, don't be frightened. I don't want you to be afraid. All I want, *really want*, is to—"

Colby viciously jerked the phone away, pressed it to his ear, while his free arm went consolingly across Lauren's shoulders, drawing a close, protective circle around her, cradling her against his chest.

What he was doing felt so natural, so right, so good. With a soft, kittenish whimper, Lauren moved deeper into his embrace, pressing her cheek against his broad chest, clinging to his warm, comforting touch without really holding him. He

36

was a rock, an island in a turbulent sea, and she wanted to stay in his hold long after he had slammed down the receiver.

Something was horribly wrong. Lauren sensed it in his withdrawal, felt it in the hands that settled on her shoulders and set her away from him. The muscles of her abdomen tightened with a resurgence of fear. Curious, needing reassurance, she lifted a searching gaze to his face, but Colby was a master at cover-up, and by this time the stiffness had gone from him and all she saw was the softening of his tanned features as his mouth smiled.

The smile didn't fool her. If anything, it seemed to heighten her suspicion that something was not right.

"What did he say, Lieutenant?"

Colby's strong shoulders sketched a brief shrug. "Nothing too interesting."

He was lying, and not very convincingly at that. Lauren looked up at him, confused. Had the threats gone from sexual harassment to threats against her life? she wondered. She found herself wishing she had not allowed him to wrench the phone from her. In her opinion, not knowing what had been said was far worse than having to endure the smutty talk to which the sicko would have subjected her.

Colby saw the light of battle entering Lauren's eyes and suspected that she was gearing herself up for a full-fledged inquiry. Not wanting to fuel her fear by getting involved in a long discussion about the foul-mouthed nuisance caller, he glanced around the room, searching for something to divert her from her intended course, and smiled when he looked at the phone.

"If you don't mind, I'd like to use your phone. For a local call," he added as an afterthought.

"Be my guest," she said. She turned to go into the kitchen, not so much because she wanted to give him privacy to make his call, but because she needed something to drink. Her throat felt scratchy.

"Could I trouble you for a glass of water?" Colby called after her, and Lauren nodded.

The instant she was out of sight, Colby hurried to Lauren's desk. Allowing himself a second's amusement as he took a close look at Freddy, he dropped down on the chair and picked up the phone. Quickly he dialed Anne's number, a number that until today he had thought he knew as well as his name.

There was no answer. He hadn't really expected Anne still to be at home, waiting for him. Nor had he expected to feel so lost. He sat staring out the window, unseeing, while the phone continued to ring, its rhythmic sound like the distant tolling of a bell.

With exaggerated care he replaced the receiver and for a few seconds stayed where he was, a remote expression in his eyes.

Tomorrow. Tomorrow, he would call Anne and apologize, he thought, and stood, rotating his head to ease the neck and shoulder muscles that had knotted with tension. He knew the love affair was over, but he wanted them to part friends. "Who the hell am I kidding?" he muttered, his mouth twisting with a sneer. Anne Mulrooney simply was not the type of woman a man like him kept around as a friend.

He walked across the room, but he slowed his pace and smiled as he came to the kitchen door.

There were two glasses filled with ice sitting on the sink counter, and Lauren was pouring water into them. Colby waited until she had set the pitcher down and then broke the comfortable silence that surrounded her.

"Would you join me for dinner?"

His sudden appearance surprised her almost as much as his invitation. Lauren whirled around, nearly upsetting the glasses with her elbow. She stared at Colby in annoyance.

His apology was charged with laughter. "I'm sorry if I startled you."

The dark glance she gave him belied the smile on her

38

mouth. "That's all right," she said. "It's just that I'm not used to having anyone sneak up on me."

He decided to ignore her snide remark in favor of asking again, "Will you join me for dinner?" He searched her face expectantly. "Unless, of course, you've already eaten," he amended. "In which case, would you join me anyway? For a cup of coffee, at least?" He smiled persuasively.

Although it was obvious he wanted company for dinner, Lauren knew she ought to refuse. And she did. "No," she said, shaking her head. And then, as if her voice had a will all its own, she heard it saying, "I haven't eaten yet. And, yes, I'd love to join you."

Satisfaction sparkled in his eyes. "Terrific! But, first, do you mind if I use your bathroom to wash up?"

"Be my guest," Lauren replied. She directed him to the guest bathroom and then went back to her glass of water, thinking that Colby had gone. She turned to go out of the kitchen and collided with him.

"Oh!" She stepped back, stretching her arm to avoid drenching herself, and splashed him as he reached out to steady her.

"I guess I'm going to need that towel sooner than I anticipated," he said, laughing as he shook off the water she had spilled onto his sleeve.

"I'm sorry!" She looked up, embarrassed.

"My fault," he insisted.

"You're right," she agreed, laughing softly.

His eyes widened. "You are kinda jumpy," he pointed out reasonably.

"Only when someone sneaks up on me," she defended, and he grinned.

"All right. It was my fault entirely. Now, where do you keep the towels?"

"You'll find whatever you need in the closet just inside the bathroom door."

"Thanks."

This time Lauren decided not to take a chance, and watched him until he had gone out of the kitchen. Only then did she consider it safe to turn toward the sink to rinse out her glass.

She mopped up the spilled water, refilled the ice trays, and returned them to the freezer. She didn't know how long Colby would take to freshen up, so she kept herself busy tidying the kitchen.

CHAPTER THREE

"Oh, my word!" Lauren whispered, pressing a hand to her mouth. She sped across the kitchen to the window, her bare feet soundless as they touched the gold linoleum. When she agreed to have dinner with the lieutenant, she had completely forgotten about her gossipy neighbor Natalia. Now, as she stood by the window, her left foot tapping steadily on the floor, she realized she had a problem.

"A doozy of one," she murmured, her gaze roving freely over the shiny black car parked in her driveway. A Porsche. Almost identical to the one that Tish's former husband had owned. Classy and very, very expensive.

There was no way that the Argus-eyed Natalia would miss that car, Lauren thought, her eyes focusing on the blue-and-white house across the street from hers.

As though the very thought of her had conjured her up, Natalia suddenly appeared on the porch. For a few moments she stood by the door, hands resting on rounded hips, attention supposedly focused on something or someone at the end of the street.

The ploy didn't fool Lauren. She knew Natalia had spied the Porsche from her living-room window and was outside to get a closer look at it.

"Damn!" Lauren hissed through her teeth. Before the evening was over, Natalia would have called all her cronies to report that she had seen still another strange car parked outside Lauren's home.

Speculation would run rife, and in the next couple of days one or two of her most nervy neighbors would approach her and subtly (or so they would think!) try to discover if the Porsche's owner was a beau or just another client.

If my nosy neighbors would only tend to their own affairs, they would be too busy to snoop into mine, she grumbled silently, a frown puckering her brow.

"Something wrong?"

Startled, Lauren spun around, her frown more pronounced. For the space of a heartbeat she held her breath. Common sense told her that Colby Sherman couldn't possibly have gotten more attractive in the short time he'd been out of her sight, but her eyes challenged that he was.

He was leaning against the doorjamb, curiously watching her. Sleeves rolled to the elbows—presumably to keep them from getting wet while he washed—exposed firmly muscled forearms that were beautifully tanned and covered with a fine layer of sun-bleached hair. His tie was gone; his shirt was opened to the third button, revealing the rounded neck of his white undershirt and a hint of dark chest hair peeking over the neckline.

Colby coughed deliberately, arresting Lauren's study of him.

Her gaze flew to his face, and recalling his question, she shook her head. "No, nothing."

"You looked preoccupied."

"I'm not." How could she explain that the woman who lived across the street spent most of her time looking out the window, spying on everyone?—that his shiny black car would give Natalia Douglas food for gossip for the next week?—that Natalia would call her parents and casually mention the unfamiliar car in the driveway and "wonder" if there was a new man in Lauren's life?

A large smile spread across Colby's features, lightly bracketing his mouth and accentuating the tiny lines that fanned outward from the corners of his eyes. His tone was half teasing, half serious. "I thought maybe you were worried that the caller was lurking around out there."

Humph! The caller's got nothing on Natalia! Lauren thought, her eyes snapping. "Oh, it's nothing like that," she said, delighting him with a gamine grin. "I was just wondering if I should wear a sweater or a jacket."

Not for a minute did Colby believe her, but he decided against prying into the reason for her frowns. "It's not cold outside," he said. "Besides, my car's pretty comfortable, and you'll be going into a diner that's usually kept very warm."

Happy to have something to divert him from his curiosity, Lauren smiled sweetly. "Where, exactly, are you taking me?"

Uh-uh-uh! What an opening! Colby's eyes gleamed with wicked delight, and he almost said, *Wherever you'll let me!* But she'd probably throw something at him. "The Dandy Diner," he answered. "It's little more than a hole in the wall, but they put out the best hot dogs in the world."

"Oh?" she inquired with a trace of challenge in her voice.

"Well, at least in this part of the world," he amended good-naturedly. "Besides," he added, his lopsided grin slightly sheepish, "it's the only place in town that still charges only forty-five cents for a cup of coffee and gives you all the refills you can drink."

Lauren nodded distractedly. She had already switched mental gears back to Natalia, who, she strongly suspected, would break all speed records spreading the word that she'd just seen Lauren getting into a car with a strange man.

Unconsciously gnawing on the corner of her lower lip while she mulled over her problem, Lauren was not aware that Colby was studying her intently. *Damn Natalia and her infernal snooping!* she thought, frowning fiercely. What in the world was she going to tell her parents when they called?

If she claimed that the Porsche's owner was a new client, she would save her parents from needless worry, but she would feel guilty for lying to them. And allowing them to believe Colby was a "friend" would be tantamount to lying.

Great choices I have, she thought sourly. Lie and feel guilty. Or tell them the truth and watch dear old Dad hem and haw about going on vacation while his "little girl" was being harassed by a sex maniac. He would probably end up canceling his vacation so he could be around "for Laurie's sake."

Hanged if I do, and hanged if I don't, Lauren thought glumly.

"If it's my car you're frowning over, let me assure you that you'll be as safe in it as you were in your baby stroller," Colby teased. "And I promise to bring you home all in one piece." *As good as you look, kitten, that's going to take some doing,* he added silently, wistfully surveying every inch of her, from her somewhat untidy hair to her slanted eyes, pert little nose, and full mouth, then went on to investigate the trim, petite body right down to the outrageously decorated toenails.

Lauren shifted nervously. The half-smile on his lips, the way his hands rested on his hips, the narrowed eyes, gave Colby Sherman a decidedly rakish air. And the way he was looking her over gave her a tingling suspicion that the gorgeous lieutenant just might be mentally undressing her.

For the first time in her adult life Lauren felt horribly self-conscious. Her first instinct was to shrink into the woodwork, but she steeled herself and gave him her softest, most provocative smile. "Actually, I was wondering if I would offend you by suggesting that I be allowed to buy dinner."

Surprise sent Colby's left eyebrow skidding upward. "I see," he said, amusement replacing the astonishment she'd seen in his eyes. "One look at my car and you've decided I need charity." With lazy, exaggerated movements he unrolled one sleeve and then the other, leaving the cuffs folded back.

In hypnotic fashion Lauren watched as he began moving

toward her, the power and grace of his movements making her pulses jump. Her breath caught, and her heart began a wild, inharmonious beating. If she allowed him to touch her, she knew she would scatter every which way, and just like poor Humpty, no one would ever be able to put Lauren Shayler together again.

Sheer instinct made her draw back and out of his reach. A semblance of normality returned when she was able to take a breath not laced with Colby's spicy cologne. Covering her cowardly act with a thin veneer of flippancy, she looked at him and mocked, "Considering that your car probably cost more than I make in a year, I'd say that you can afford to pick up the tab more than I can. But since I've obviously inconvenienced you, the least I can do is buy your dinner."

"I'm from the old school," Colby murmured, increasing her agitation by deliberately decreasing the distance between them. "ERA proponents despair of me," he went on, his voice soft and seductive, "but I hold to the cavalier notion that if I invite a beautiful woman out, I take care of the check."

Oh, Lordy, you do know all the right words, don't you? Lauren thought shakily, struggling to take a deep breath while her heart seemed to be doing a wild dance in the middle of her throat. "I'd really feel a whole lot better if you let me buy," she said, her voice embarrassingly breathless. Striving to hold on to the pitiful shreds of her composure, she forced her eyes up to his face.

His amused expression had vanished, and for a millisecond Lauren saw displeasure clearly stamped over his ruggedly handsome features. Then his perfect white teeth were bared in a smile that increased her emotional discomfort.

"I make it a practice never to argue with a featherweight." The mocking intonation he employed was in direct variance with the intense look in his eyes as they made a slow, thorough inspection of her features.

Air, she thought. *I need a breath of fresh air.* "Shall we go?" Lauren suggested, feigning a coolness she was far from feeling.

Colby's eyes glittered strangely as they surveyed her from head to toe, his gaze lingering on her feet. "Aren't you forgetting something?" he asked in a mild, questioning voice that carried a faint thread of amusement.

Lauren glanced down and immediately understood the source of his merriment. Her bare feet. She was so used to running about without shoes, she might have left the house without them if he hadn't reminded her she was barefoot.

"I'll be with you in a moment," she mumbled, and then she skirted around him and tried not to run as she left the kitchen.

You're behaving like a klutzy adolescent, she berated herself silently as she walked into the living room for her gray suede leather boots and matching bag. *Blushing, twitching nervously, running away like a scared rabbit!* she thought disgustedly. *Honestly! You'd think you'd never seen a sexy man before!*

In fact, she hadn't. At least not as handsome, as virile, as imposing, as the one she had left in the kitchen. Lauren sighed as she picked up a boot and balanced on one foot to slip it on.

Colby had not stayed in the kitchen. He had come in behind her and was enjoying an unobstructed view of the back of her thighs as Lauren bent over, pulling on the boot.

He blinked, gave a vigorous shake of his head to clear it. "Do you need any help?" he asked amusedly. He felt like a peeping Tom but he couldn't help himself. His fingers itched to caress her exposed skin, to delight in the silken feel of her thighs.

Startled, Lauren trembled out of balance, and Colby rushed across the room to prevent her from falling. Like electric shocks prickling her skin, tiny shivers skittered up her arm as his strong, warm fingers gripped her elbow. She had to fight to keep herself from jerking free of his hold

46

while at the same time she valiantly struggled against a heady impulse to lean into him.

She had to clear her throat before she could speak, but even then she managed a barely audible "Thank you," as with his help she finished pulling on her boots.

"You're quite welcome," Colby said, smiling because he knew why her voice was so low. It was certainly nice knowing that he was not the only one affected when he touched her.

They went out, and Lauren breathed a sigh of relief when she turned back to lock the front door because it gave her the excuse she needed to break free of Colby's much-too-thrilling hold.

As she was standing by the Porsche, waiting for Colby to open her door, Lauren remembered Natalia. She hazarded a glance across the street and cringed. Just as she had suspected, and dreaded, Natalia was still on the porch, openly watching them.

Even as she was succumbing to a childish urge, Lauren realized it was unworthy of her. She lifted a hand and gaily waved to the woman, almost immediately dropping the guilty hand to her mouth to stifle a fit of giggles brought on by Natalia's sudden discomfiture. In her haste to duck into the house, Natalia turned too sharply and almost crashed against the door when her foot caught the ragged hem of her faded blue chenille robe.

"In you go," Colby said, throwing open the car door. He took her arm and helped her into the car.

As she made herself comfortable on the black leather seat, Lauren began to regret having called the police. But only because of the mischief Natalia's gossiping would cause her.

Drat the woman! she thought with a hostility that left her breathless. She respected her neighbors' privacy, so why was it so hard for Natalia, and others like her, to show her the same courtesy? She leaned back with a sigh of exasperation and closed her eyes.

Colby slanted a glance at her as he was backing onto the street, and noticed the two tiny vertical furrows that seemed to have been penciled in between her eyebrows.

"Headache?" he questioned, deftly shifting gears.

"Not really. My eyes are just tired." Her frown deepened. Since this man had entered her home, she had done more lying than she remembered doing in all her twenty-six years.

"A cold, damp towel applied while the lids are closed will do wonders for mild eyestrain," he offered helpfully. Lauren merely sighed. He grinned. "A good night's sleep was what I would suggest after that. Looks to me like maybe you haven't been getting enough sleep."

Nice going, Sherlock! Lauren mocked silently. Since the calls had started, she had become a very light sleeper and wakened abruptly with the slightest provocation.

"I'll make sure you get home early," he said.

There was a ring of disappointment in his quiet voice. She saw that he was frowning but dared not ask why, although she was vastly curious.

"I'll appreciate that," she murmured.

Some ten minutes later Colby drove into the parking lot behind the Dandy Diner and parked his Porsche between two patrol cars. He frowned as he killed the engine and removed the key from the ignition with some reluctance, his gaze shifting restlessly over the woman beside him. He was plagued by an inexplicable reluctance to share her with his friends.

Sensing his hesitation, Lauren turned to look into the diner. Immediately her brow furrowed. A cop hangout. Out of the corner of her eye she sneaked a look at Colby, wondering if this was one of his "haunts."

It very probably is, she thought with a rueful grimace.

"Are we eating out or in?" she asked, twisting around to look at Colby. He was staring almost fixedly at the hood of his car.

48

"If you'd rather, I'll go get the hot dogs and we can take them back to your house." He sounded hopeful.

Not a good idea. "I'd rather eat here. If you don't mind."

"Of course not." He opened his door and came around to help her out of the car. He felt compelled to warn her about the men who belonged to the squad cars scattered about the parking lot. "There're a few friends of mine in there. Nice guys, but they tend to get carried away. Don't take anything they say too seriously."

What was it he was afraid of? Lauren wondered, eyeing him curiously. "Don't worry about me, Lieutenant," she said, laughing softly. "Us cynics believe nothing of what we hear and only half of what we see," she added, her eyes glittering with amusement.

He was not amused. "You're much too young to be a cynic."

That was debatable, but Lauren allowed his remark to go unchallenged. She slipped the strap of her purse across one shoulder and started moving toward the diner.

A group of teenaged girls in soccer uniforms were approaching from the opposite direction, and as they all came together at the door, Colby lost Lauren. Smaller than most of the athletic teenagers, Lauren was accidentally absorbed into their group, and they were much too busy laughing and rehashing the finer points of the game they'd just won to notice it.

Willy-nilly, Lauren was swept into the crowded diner, but she managed to slip away when the girls scattered, some to go to the counter, some to find the ladies' room, and some, like her, to find a table. She was relieved to find a table for two at the far end of the room that was thankfully far away from where the girls finally settled.

She saw Colby searching the room, presumably looking for her, but it was too crowded for him to see her if she waved and much too noisy for her voice to carry. Lauren decided her only option was to wait for him to find her.

Giggling, chattering like magpies, shoving each other, and generally enjoying themselves, the girls gathered at the counter to order. But the beautiful redhead behind the counter hardly noticed them and directed herself to Colby at the door. "I was wondering if you'd gotten too good for us now that you're no longer in uniform," she called out in a voice that, to Lauren, seemed deliberately provocative.

Colby laughed and shook his head. Before he could answer, a rough male voice taunted, "Stood up again, Lieutenant?"

A chorus of teasing jeers followed, and then in a voice that carried clearly over the din, a middle-aged officer piped, "Looks like Mulrooney's finally come to her senses and dumped the big ape."

Colby seemed to cringe, and the look he flashed around the room made Lauren suspect he was worried that she had heard and would want to know who this Mulrooney was. When he finally noticed her, she pretended innocence and, smiling, waved to him.

Looking relieved, Colby began to move toward her, unaware that the man who had referred to him as "the big ape" was following closely at his heels.

"I thought I'd lost you," Colby whispered, lowering his long body onto the padded stool. His mouth crooked with a smile that vanished the minute he became aware of his "shadow."

The man had a jolt when he saw Lauren. His jaw literally dropped. "Oh, wow!" he whispered, awed. "I can see why Anne's history!"

Anne. The name echoed reminiscently in Lauren's mind. Her eyes narrowed contemplatively, and she searched Colby's tight-jawed expression long moments before his low voice broke her concentration.

"Lauren Shayler, this is Peter Demarest." There was a definite lack of interest as he made the introductions.

"Pleased to meet you," they chorused. Peter's voice was

throbbing with curiosity; Lauren's was soft and polite. After a few minutes, during which he stared at Lauren but spoke to Colby, Peter Demarest excused himself and returned to his seat.

Lauren wasted no time. Clasping her hands, she leaned forward, and in a tight little whisper challenged, "Repeat after me: 'Anne, darling, I'm very sorry that I'm so late in calling.'" She propped her elbows on the white Formica table and rested her chin on her folded hands, her eyes unblinkingly, unamusedly, fixed on Colby's sheepish expression.

"Guilty as charged," he murmured, and had the good grace to blush.

"'Dizzy broad'!" her eyes glinted mutinously as she mimicked him. "You said I got my kicks from answering pay phones!"

"Would it help if I asked forgiveness on bended knees?"

"It wouldn't hurt!"

His eyes widened. "You wouldn't be so cruel."

Her eyes narrowed. "Don't bet on it!"

He grinned. "I'm not a betting man."

She glared. "Even if you were, you'd lose."

"When you answered my first wrong number, you seemed like such a softhearted, compassionate soul," he reminded her gently, running the tip of his forefinger across the top of her knuckles. "Don't tell me I made an error in judgment."

Lauren pulled her hand away, somehow maintaining her unsmiling façade. "It wouldn't be your first one today."

Colby visibly winced. "Do you always go for the jugular?"

"Whenever necessary, Lieutenant."

"You must have trouble keeping friends that way."

What she was having trouble keeping was a straight face. But she somehow managed. "With friends I tend to be merciful. With enemies I tend to be just. It's the clowns that hang in limbo who need to watch out for my claws."

He made a big production out of rolling up one sleeve,

then looked up at her, his eyes twinkling, and asked, "Would you mind initiating me where it won't show?"

Their laughter exploded in unison, and it stopped abruptly when the redheaded waitress demanded, "Sherman, are you going to order or not?" Her cheeks were rosy from the heat of the steamers. As she stood by their table, tapping her foot, her hands balled and resting on her slim hips, Lauren got the impression that she was not happy with the lieutenant.

After a quick, disdainful look at Lauren, the redhead turned back to Colby. "This time you're going to pay."

Lauren lifted a quizzical gaze to the waitress's face and came up against cold, hard eyes that left her in no doubt that she was the source of the redhead's bad humor.

Draw in your claws, lady, she thought crossly, and turned away from the woman's dour expression, leaving Colby to order for both of them and to settle his differences with the waitress as best he could.

Was this one of the women Colby sought solace from when "darling Anne" was not available? Lauren studied the reflection of Colby's face in the window, and noted that he was smiling. He had a charming smile and knew how to use it, she thought, feeling strangely vexed by that smile.

At last the hazel-eyed vixen moved away, and Colby cleared his throat to gain Lauren's attention.

"Tell me about yourself," he prompted.

"There's not much to tell," she hedged.

"Of course there is," he insisted. Propping an elbow on the table, he leaned his face into his palm and devoted all his attention to her.

"You know where I live, and no doubt already figured out that I live alone. I own my answering service, and run it with the help of a high-school girl who comes in two afternoons a week and all day Saturday. I'm twenty-six, not independently wealthy, and happily single."

"With no thought to changing that status?" he murmured, his eyes becoming intent on her mouth.

Lauren's eyes gleamed with amusement. "Oh, I think of it all the time!" She waited for his reaction, and her amusement increased in direct proportion to the interest she detected in his expression. "And since I'm already independent, all I need is to get the wealthy part."

"You're outrageous," he claimed. *Delightfully so,* he thought.

Just then the waitress reappeared. She slapped their hot dogs on the table and spilled the coffee as she was pouring it because she was too busy glaring at Colby.

Lauren forced herself to say, "Thank you," as a couple of napkins were flung on the table. *And thank God for little favors,* she added silently as the woman whirled away.

When they were finally alone Lauren began to enjoy being with Colby. He was sharp witted, and charming, and he seemed to be going out of his way to make her laugh.

Though off and on she was aware of a laugh, the buzz of party chatter, or the whine of a child who was tired and irritable, Lauren felt as if there were just the two of them alone in the room. She had eyes only for Colby, and he for her.

The spell was broken when Colby innocently removed a dab of mustard from the corner of her mouth with his thumb. Lauren blinked in surprise and instinctively jerked back, away from the hand that was again reaching toward her face.

Trembling fingers picked up a napkin and took it up to her face, quickly wiped the corners of her mouth, and then crumpled it out of sheer nervousness.

Darn him! Lauren was mortified when she felt her face becoming warm under his steady, somewhat mocking regard. "Have I got more mustard on my face?" she demanded, glaring at him.

"A bit here"—gently rubbing her chin—"and a dab here"

—touching the undercurve of her lower lip with the tip of his index finger.

You wicked man! she silently fumed, but she could not deny the little thrill that rushed through her body, nor the warm feeling that lingered as his fingers trailed over her chin.

"If you've finished?" Slowly, Colby unfolded his long body from the pink vinyl stool and stretched.

Poor guy, she thought. He was tired and didn't seem to have the energy to hide it.

She waited until they were in the car before she ventured, "If you'd rather go on home, I can call a taxi to take me home." She smiled wanly. "I'm sure I'll be all right."

Her voice lacked conviction. Colby was both touched and amused by her false bravado. He started the car, then turned to look at her.

"Are you in that much of a hurry to get rid of me?"

She hesitated for a moment. "Not really," she admitted.

"I'm glad."

As the car was moving slowly out of the parking lot, Lauren turned to look out the window. The sky was almost black, and there was no moon.

Was it going to rain again? she wondered, and found herself wishing for a heavy downpour that would cancel tomorrow's softball game. She would rather be lazy and stay in bed until noon.

"Where are we going?" she asked, suddenly aware that they were not headed back to her house.

"I'm taking you home," Colby replied casually.

Whose home? she wanted to ask, but instead, she straightened in the seat and peered through the windshield. It was too dark to see the street signs, and she couldn't recognize any landmarks. "This isn't the way back," she stated, her firm voice faintly tinged with concern.

"Maybe not the shortest way back, but this is certainly one way to get there."

"Oh" sounded so inane, yet she could think of nothing else to say.

It had taken approximately ten minutes to get to the diner, but as Colby pulled into her driveway, Lauren sneaked a glance at her wristwatch and noticed that the return trip had taken almost half an hour.

Colby set the emergency brake, but didn't kill the engine. He sat for a moment with his hands gripping the steering wheel, his eyes focused on the dark outline of her house. Finally, he turned to Lauren.

"How about if I come in with you to check the house?"

"I don't want to impose. . . ." Lauren felt her pulses jump as Colby reached out and pressed the tips of two fingers across her lips to silence her.

"It's no imposition," he murmured. His eyes seemed to pick up the glow from the dashboard lights and glinted as he sat there just looking at her. For a moment their eyes locked and held. In his lurked desire. Hers were overbright with a mixture of yearning and apprehension.

Unnerved by the silence, Lauren mumbled, "I'd better go in. I have a very busy day tomorrow." She had started to reach for the handle when he leaned across her and opened the door. She held her breath, willing him to move away before she humiliated herself by touching the face that was so temptingly close.

At last he straightened up, but the tangy scent of his cologne lingered, and Lauren inhaled it when she finally was able to take a deep breath.

If she didn't come apart at the seams before he was through with her, it wouldn't be for lack of trying on his part, Lauren thought, following Colby's movements as he left the car. Just looking at the man made her tingle all the way down to the tips of her toes.

By the time Colby came around to her door, Lauren was all sweetness and light. She smiled up at him as he took her hand to help her from the car. "Thank you, kind sir," she said, laughing softly.

"My pleasure," he murmured.

When she opened the front door, he leaned close to her ear and told her to wait for him there. An involuntary, uncontrollable shiver spread a pleasant, albeit temporary, warmth through Lauren's slender body, and she was able only to nod in response to his whispered instruction.

Satisfied there was no intruder waiting to pounce on Lauren inside the house, Colby returned to tell her he was going to check the outside. Lauren nodded and stayed where she was until he came back to her.

"Is it all right if I turn on the light now?" she whispered. His cloak-and-dagger behavior had left her with a dry throat and an uneasy feeling in the pit of her stomach. She knew that once she turned on a few lights, the familiarity of her surroundings would bring immediate relief.

A few minutes later she was in full possession of her normal self.

"Would you like a cup of coffee or something?"

"As much as I'd like to say yes, I can't," he said, casting a wistful glance at the couch. "Unless I get some sleep very soon, I'm going to fall flat on my face." He stood for a moment looking down at her without moving a muscle. And then he smiled tiredly. "I'll check on you tomorrow," he promised.

"I'd appreciate that."

Appreciate. Colby would have much preferred to hear her saying that she would like to see him again. "Until tomorrow, then," he said softly.

There was a strange quality in his voice, but Lauren attributed it to weariness. Wordlessly, she opened the door for him.

"Be sure to lock and bolt it," he ordered, tapping his knuckles on the door. He went on out to the porch and waited until he'd heard the deadbolt clicking into place.

56

"Good night, Lauren," he called through the door.

"Good night, Lieutenant Sherman," she returned, smiling as she turned her back to the door. Tomorrow, she thought dreamily. Tomorrow, he would call or come to see her. And after that—

She threw open the door again and ran outside to tell him that she was not going to be home on Saturday, but he was already gone.

"Rats!" She spun around and walked back into the house, her head bowed dejectedly.

CHAPTER FOUR

Saturday morning was cloudy, but there was no rain to cancel out the game. At ten Lauren trudged out into the living room in a fleece robe and matching turquoise slippers, mumbled a greeting to the perky little brunette at the switchboard, and went on into the kitchen.

Thank goodness for conscientious employees like Maggie, she thought, heading for the coffeepot like a bee to a pittosporum plant. Every Saturday at seven Maggie would let herself into the house, tiptoe into the kitchen, and make the coffee. The first cup was hers. She took it to the switchboard, along with one of the two breakfast pastries she usually brought.

Smiling with satisfaction, Lauren took a bite of her pastry. It was wonderful the way she and Maggie had taken to each other from their first meeting. When the career counselor at her old alma mater had told her she was sending a sophomore for her to interview, Lauren's first impulse was to say, *Forget it*. But, because the counselor was an old friend, she had silently reserved the right to refuse to hire the girl and agreed to the interview. She'd hired Maggie that first day and had never regretted it.

Sipping the coffee as she walked, she went into the living room.

Maggie glanced up as Lauren entered the room, her brown eyes twinkling. "You don't look quite awake yet," she observed, laughing. "But maybe that's the best time to give you your messages," she went on, shuffling papers on the table until she found the ones she wanted. "Ah, here they are." She fanned the notes and started reading. "One, your father called. He sounded impatient, so I guess he wasn't very happy about me answering the phone instead of you. He wants you to call him back ASAP!"

Lauren groaned. Maggie glanced up, grinned, and went on. "Two, Tish cannot come to dinner tomorrow. Date with Larry Somebody-or-other." She turned pink as she tried to keep herself from giggling, and failed. "Doesn't she even bother to find out the guy's last name before she goes out with him?"

Lauren shrugged. "Anyone else call?" she prompted, both hoping and dreading to hear that Colby had called and she had missed him.

"Your grandmother. She will be here for dinner and said that she would bring—I can't figure out what she said 'cause she was talking too fast."

"Probably piroshkis." Lauren grinned and stepped back to lean against the wall. She curled her hands around the coffee mug. "That's what she usually brings, because she doesn't think I eat right, so she'll make enough to feed an army and then fill my little freezer with the leftovers."

Maggie flashed her an impish smile. "Your coach called too. Said for you not to forget the oranges this time."

"I think I'll take the oranges and forget me this time," Lauren threatened, pushing away from the wall with a sigh. "I sure don't feel like playing today." At least, not softball, she amended. One hazel-eyed, tawny-haired police lieutenant came swiftly to mind as a likely partner for some very interesting indoor sports.

With that thought in mind, and a silly little grin on her mouth, Lauren went to the kitchen to refill her cup. She took that cup to the bedroom to drink while she dressed.

Her hair went up in crisscrossed braids, the only sensible hairdo for the rough workout ahead. She dresssed in brown

59

sweats and matching tennis shoes. A wide brown sweatband went around her head as an accessory, but would later prove a wonderful restraint, as her hair usually didn't stay in the braids throughout the game.

"Look at you," Maggie remarked, smiling with amusement when Lauren returned to the living room. "You look more like you're off to a picnic than to a ball game."

Lauren moaned dramatically. "If only I were!" For a moment she stared at her personal phone, debating whether or not to leave a message with Maggie in case Colby called. Deciding against it, she hurried into the kitchen for the oranges and, as she was heading for the front door, told Maggie only that she would try to be home by three.

"Don't worry about it. I brought my books with me. Mom's being a rag—" She stopped abruptly when Lauren turned and gave her a sharp look. "Well, she's upset with me because she doesn't like my math grade and she says that it's because I don't study enough."

"Which is probably true," Lauren scolded with mock severity. "The calculator's in my desk drawer. You're welcome to borrow it if you need it."

Mom's being a rag echoed in her mind as she went into the garage. *Rag.* Lauren smiled with wry amusement. These days "bad" meant good, and "gay" was bad. Boys who didn't appeal were "geeks," or, in some extreme cases, "jocks." And, at least in Jill's vocabulary, the young males who weren't geeks or jocks were "fine."

"How'd it go?" Maggie asked when Lauren came hobbling into the living room at half past two that afternoon.

"Miserably." Muscles she'd forgotten she had protested with each tentative step she took toward the sofa. "I played my worst game ever! Struck out twice, once when the bases were loaded." She balled up her fist and held it up in mock triumph. "Singlehandedly, I lost the game." With a shamefaced grin she added, "At least, that's the impression I got from the coach and the rest of the team." She dropped down on the sofa with a dramatic groan.

"Well, I'm sure Mudville will survive, Mighty Casey," an amused male voice teased from somewhere behind her.

Colby! Setting aside her low spirits and forgetting her aching muscles, Lauren jumped from the couch, in the same movement turning to face the man who had so dominated her thoughts she had swung at balls even when they were high and outside.

He was standing at the door to the kitchen, a bottle of beer in his hand, a smile on his mouth, and a devilish glint in his eyes.

"Drinking on duty, Lieutenant?" Lauren asked with a touch of disapproval in her soft voice.

He smiled with only one corner of his mouth. "Maggie offered this as a bribe, to keep me from ticketing her the next time I see her out on the highways," he explained, lifting the bottle, "because she wouldn't tell me where you were playing." His eyes literally danced with amusement. "I'da gone to watch the game, if only to cheer you on."

"Remind me to give you a bonus," Lauren said to Maggie. "The very last thing I needed today was a cheering section." She lifted her eyes to Colby and realized that he seemed more interested in studying her than in what she was saying. Even before she glanced down at herself, she knew she looked like something the cat had dragged in and abandoned when he'd come to his senses. Caked mud on her knees, thighs, and elbows was silent testimony to the times she had either tried to slide to safety or taken a fall.

Colby gazed at her, remembering something his grandfather had once told him: *It's easy to desire a woman who looks good, but a man knows he's in real trouble when he finds himself wanting a woman when she isn't at her best. Grandfather, am I in trouble!* Even with her hair in total disarray, and her face spotted with dried mud, Lauren Shayler was one sexy woman!

"I'm off duty at five," he said. "Do you think you can be ready for dinner by six?" If he played his cards right, she would be his dessert.

Maggie was watching them with avid interest. She couldn't count the times she had heard Lauren turning down dates with men who she said were "all ego." Usually with a sneer.

"Are you inviting me to dinner, Lieutenant?" The smile on Lauren's face was as false as the sweetness of her tone. She had never appreciated the "masterful" type.

A warning bell clanged in his brain, and Colby prudently heeded it. "Yes, I am," he drawled in a silky-smooth tone. Lauren's eyes widened briefly, and he smiled, suspecting his answer had caught her by surprise. "And if six is too early, we can make it at seven." His grin was disarming, and Lauren felt her annoyance with his high-handedness slowly dissipating.

"Six will be fine."

"I'll see you at six, then." Winking at Maggie, Colby set the beer bottle down by the television set, said his good-byes, and promptly left.

"For a minute there I thought you were going to send him packing," Maggie remarked the second the door had closed behind Colby. "And that would've been a shame, because that guy's super fine!"

Lauren laughed. "Yes, he is, isn't he?" A feeling of unreality gripped her as she started moving away. From living room to bedroom, bedroom to bathroom, she went over the brief encounter with Colby. There was nothing she hated worse than an arrogant male, and yet, here she was, tingling with anticipated pleasure at being with Colby Sherman again. Pulling off her dirty clothes, she bunched them and threw them into the hamper, and then turned the faucets on full blast over the tub.

Sweet relief tingled upward from her tender toes as she stepped into the hot bath. With single-minded purpose she concentrated on relaxing her abused muscles, and managed to keep Colby from entering her thoughts.

Later, dressed in matching blue bra and bikini briefs, she sat in front of her makeup mirror—brush in one hand and hot iron in the other—and stared with skeptical eyes at her image. What was she doing? Primping for a man who, doubtless, was spreading himself too thinly already, trying to juggle his free time between "darling Anne" and the redhead at the Dandy Diner?

"Variety is the spice of life, or so they say," she told her reflection in the glass. "So, what say we make the lieutenant's life a *lot* spicier?" She grinned wickedly at her reflection, then went to work on her hair. What she didn't want to admit, even to herself, was that she wanted to be with Colby, no matter how many women had claim to his time.

"You look great!" Maggie approved with a good-natured grin when Lauren wandered into the living room a few minutes before five.

"Don't sound so surpised!" Lauren's eyes twinkled with humor. "I dress up once in a while." She was wearing a blue linen shift that could be dressed up with red pumps and red accessories if Colby decided to take her somewhere other than to the Dandy Diner. If, however, he was casually dressed, she would wear her low-heeled white sandals and complement them with the white-shell necklace her parents had brought her from Hawaii.

"Yeah, but not quite like that," Maggie countered with a crooked grin as she tidied up her work space. It was time for her to go home. "You must want to impress the lieutenant."

"Maybe." Lauren crossed the room, picked up Maggie's telephone log, glanced over it, then set it back down with a satisfied smile. "Looks like business is really picking up for Stewart's Accounting."

"It's about time," Maggie rejoined with spirit. "Greg Stewart told me he was getting ready to go to Valley so that he could get a full-time job to help out. His mom was getting very discouraged because no one wanted to give her a break. And she's really good."

"That, I suppose, is Greg's unbiased opinion?" Lauren teased, and Maggie blushed. "I'm glad that Greg won't have to quit school to get a job."

"So am I!" Maggie laughed as she reached under the table for her purse and books. "I'll see you Monday afternoon, all right?"

"Fine. Oh!" Monday would be the first day she had to look after the Hunter children. "I'm having company Monday."

"Oh, really? Who?"

"Jill and Donnie."

"Lucky you!" Laughing, Maggie hurried out of the house.

"Brat!" Lauren called out as she went into the kitchen. She poured a glass of wine and took it to her desk. For a few seconds she sat staring at Freddy, wondering whether or not to return her father's call. She knew why he'd called, and she really didn't feel up to answering his questions about "the strange man" she'd gone out with last night.

But as nothing could be gained by ignoring his call, she picked up the phone and dialed. "All right, Papa-san, here's your chance to treat me like a six-year-old again," she whispered.

When her mother answered on the third ring, Lauren was tempted to talk to her for a few minutes about nonsensical things, such as tomorrow's dinner menu, and then hang up. It would be cowardly, but—

"Hi, Ma, it's me."

"Hello, Me," her mother's happy voice responded. "Your father's been waiting all day for you to call back, so I won't hold you up."

"But—" was all Lauren got out before she heard her father's gravelly voice saying, "Laurie, I'm glad you finally called, honey. I've been worried sick about you."

"Why?" Lauren demanded, frowning.

"One of your neighbors called Mama last night, and said that she'd seen a strange man forcing you into his car." He cleared his throat and then went on. "I thought you were staying home last night?"

Too late, Lauren recalled that she'd turned down her parents' dinner invitation last night on the pretext of staying home to catch up on her bookkeeping. She wrinkled her nose. "Sorry, Daddy. I thought I was going to be busy, but then Colby came by and"—she forced a laugh—"well, what can I say?" *That won't be an outright lie?* she continued to herself.

His laugh was happy, relaxed. "I see. I was replaced by a younger man."

"Only for the evening, Papa," Lauren assured him.

"That's what Mama said it was," he admitted, and Lauren chuckled. If she knew her mother—and she did!—Papa was in for a little ribbing, and at least one I-told-you-so!

"So when do we get to meet your young man?"

That caught her right between the eyes. Lauren sagged and leaned both elbows on her desk to support her unsmiling face on her hands. She felt as if she'd been flattened by a steamroller. But she recovered, took a sip of wine, and promised, "I'll introduce him to you the first chance I get. You are coming here for dinner tomorrow?"

"Depends on what you're planning to feed me."

"Whatever Mom and Jeanne are bringing. I'm responsible only for the drinks and dessert. So what would you like for dessert?"

"Raspberry sorbet," they both chorused, and both laughed.

"If it's not too much trouble for you, honey," he said, and Lauren smiled with indulgence. She had been making his favorite dessert since she was old enough to know it was one way to put him into a receptive mood for some of her more outrageous requests.

"No trouble at all," she assured him, and promised him a double serving just before they said good-bye.

"Whew!" Lauren let Freddy fall to his holder and wandered over to the sofa, settling down into it with a disgruntled sigh. A half-lie. That's what she'd told her father, but even that was threatening to backfire on her. She knew her father; he would not forget about Colby and would prick her with reminders whenever it suited him. Distracted by her thoughts, she hardly tasted the wine as she sipped it.

A soothing warmth spread through her body, and slowly, Lauren began to relax. She closed her eyes and rested her head on the armrest, keeping one hand tightly curled around her wineglass to keep it from spilling even one precious drop.

Lauren hadn't realized just how fatigued she was until she began to experience a wonderful, soothing sense of weightlessness. She jerked up to a sitting position.

She had to stay awake. She could not afford to have Colby catch her napping. So she stood up and went into the kitchen to the sink to rinse her glass. Grasping a paper towel from the rack, she was in the process of wiping the water she'd spilled around the sink when the door chime rang.

With a big smile on her face Lauren dashed to the door, curled her hand around the knob, and froze. She grimaced with self-disgust. *This is ridiculous,* she thought. She couldn't go through life being afraid to open the door.

A slight tremor of apprehension was in her voice as she demanded, "Who's there?"

"Are you going to third-degree me again?" Colby demanded with mock sternness.

Lauren unlocked the door, pulled it open. Looking trim and muscular in snug-fitting, black brushed denim jeans and matching velour turtleneck, Colby stood on the porch, his arms folded across his chest. He was a knockout, pure and simple.

"May I come in?" he inquired with a grin. "Or are you going to keep me waiting on the porch again?"

"I thought that's where you did your best investigating," she quipped, but stepped aside to let him in.

"Actually, I prefer to work undercover," he said in his most suggestive, husky tone. His lips twitched as he strolled past her.

Carefully shutting the door, she leaned against it. "Would you like a drink before we leave?"

"If I say yes, we might never get to dinner," he warned in a deliberately soft voice. Before she could anticipate him, he had brought her up against his hard, muscular chest. Lauren had time only to murmur a halfhearted "Oh!" before Colby's firm mouth covered hers. An odd, tingling sensation traversed the length of her body, and again she felt a warmth spreading through her.

"We'd better get going before I decide the hell with dinner," he murmured against her lips, setting her away when Lauren would rather have stayed in his embrace.

For a moment she felt a strong sense of loss. But it ended when he carefully brushed a wispy tendril from her cheek and then fixed it firmly behind her ear.

"You're a devil, Mr. Grinch," she teased in a voice that was husky with emotion.

His laughter was equally husky. "I never claimed to be an angel," he countered, running a finger very lightly across her cheek.

"I'll just get my shoes and bag," she whispered, stepping away from him with obvious reluctance.

"That might help."

Hurrying into the bedroom, Lauren quickly stepped into her red pumps and draped a red bead necklace around her neck. She glanced into the mirror to assure herself that her hair looked all right, then grabbed her earrings and put them on as she was walking back to the living room.

"That was quick," Colby said, and Lauren smiled.

"Since I don't enjoy being kept waiting, I try not to make others wait for me," she explained, handing him her house key as they started moving toward the door.

"I hope you like Mexican."

"What happens if I say I don't?"

Colby grinned. "In that case I suppose we have no choice but to go back to the Dandy Diner."

Perish the thought! "Did I tell you that I simply love Mexican food?"

"I figured that's what you'd say." His voice was low, amused, and as he closed her door, Lauren heard him laughing.

"Have you had any more calls?" he asked as he settled in behind the wheel.

"No, thank goodness."

He nodded sagely. "I think that once you have a new number, the calls will stop completely."

"I hope you're right."

So did he.

As the car moved out of her driveway, Lauren curiously glanced across the street at Natalia's house. A light was on in what she knew was the kitchen, and the living room was dark. But she thought she saw the woman peeking out her window. She sighed dispiritedly.

"Something bothering you?"

"Only my stomach," she lied. "It's reminding me that all I've had today is a light breakfast, an orange, and a glass of wine."

"Is that a good diet for Mudville's finest slugger?"

" 'Mudville' might just lose one smart-alecky police lieutenant if he's not careful," she warned, maintaining an unsmiling expression despite the charming, infectious grin that curved one corner of Colby's mouth.

"Touchy, are we?"

"We are."

"Scratch softball," he said. "So what do we talk about that isn't a sore subject?"

"Let's talk about you."

"My most unfavorite subject. I'd much rather talk about you."

As much as she wanted to mimick his words, Lauren resisted the urge. "Tell me about this restaurant we're going to. Is it another one of your haunts?"

"As a matter of fact, no." One hand went up to comb his fingers through his hair. A stubborn strand fell across his forehead, and Lauren practically had to sit on her hands to prevent herself from smoothing it back in place.

Something on the road made him brake suddenly, and though Lauren was belted in, she was jolted forward. The cassettes that had been sitting on the dashboard fell onto her lap, eliciting a startled yelp from Lauren. Believing she was hurt, Colby quickly swerved toward the side of the road and brought the Porsche to a slow, rolling stop.

"Are you hurt?" He unbuckled his seat belt and leaned toward her, immediately the professional as he made a thorough inspection of her upper body and neck.

Not totally convinced he wasn't taking advantage of the situation, Lauren shoved him away. "I'm not hurt," she shouted, laughing with a mixture of embarrassment and nervousness. As his hands had moved over her to check for injuries, she had experienced that old familiar tingling sensation.

"Then why the devil did you scream?"

"I didn't scream! I was surprised when your tapes fell across my lap, but I did not scream."

Colby scowled and pulled himself away from her. He restarted the car, got it back on the highway, and concentrated on his driving, leaving Lauren to her own thoughts.

Which was perfectly fine with Lauren. She needed the silence almost as much as she needed the breath of fresh air

69

she inhaled deeply when he helped her out of the car half an hour later.

The parking lot was nearly full, and there were people standing in a queue outside the restaurant doors. Lauren flashed a quick glance up at Colby, a question in her eyes.

"No problem," he said. "It's always like this, but I never have to wait long." He smiled. "We can wait in the bar."

They didn't wait long.

To Lauren, dinner was a happy daze. For all the attention Colby paid the other diners, they might as well have been alone in the restaurant.

While conversation and laughter swirled around them, Colby reached across the table and took up her hand. "How come I never ran into you before, Lauren?"

"Just lucky, I guess," she teased, but he didn't smile.

"Is there anyone who has a prior claim on you?"

"Not lately." She felt his strong, virile fingers closing around her hand, and she lifted her eyes to his face. "How about you? Is there anyone who has a prior claim to you?"

He withdrew his hand, curled his fingers around his napkin, and looked uncomfortable. "No, there's not," he finally said darkly.

Lauren gazed at him thoughtfully, wondering how to ask about Anne Mulrooney. But her opportunity was lost when the waitress interrupted to ask if they wished anything else.

"Just a bit more coffee," Colby said, shifting to reach into his back pocket for his wallet. He opened it, slipped out a couple of bills, and dropped them onto the tray with the check.

The waitress picked up the tray and, saying, "I'll be right back with your change and the coffee," disappeared.

Colby leaned back, his hands curled around his coffee cup. "How did you get started with your answering service?"

"I had worked a hospital switchboard while I was in college, so when my job with the library was phased out four years ago, I decided to go into business for myself. Since I

70

couldn't very well open a library, I decided to start an answering service."

"And for four years you've been very quietly operating your business a couple miles away from where I work, and we never met."

She smiled. "If it hadn't been for that miserable caller, we might never have met."

He winked, and smiled. "In that case we just might owe a vote of thanks to him."

Thanks wasn't exactly what she'd like to give to the joker. "Boiling him in oil comes to mind as a fitting way to show my thanks," she said with a twisted smile.

"Remind me never to get on your bad side."

"I don't have a bad side."

He grinned. Glancing up at the waitress as she refreshed his coffee, he whispered a thank-you and then resumed his quiet study of Lauren.

"What are you planning for tomorrow? Another ball game?"

"Heaven forbid." She feigned a shiver. "I'm having my folks over for dinner."

"Ah . . ."

She probably would never know what prompted her to ask him to join them, but she did.

Colby's eyebrows arched, and a spark of surprise danced in his eyes. "Are you certain I wouldn't be intruding?"

"In fact, you might just get me off the hook with my dad—"

"Oh, I've never been any good with fathers."

"I don't believe it!" She started to laugh, then quickly sobered. "Actually, maybe I do. And maybe I know why too."

His brows drew together, then arched, and his eyes sparkled with amusement. "Shame on you for thinking such wicked thoughts of me," he scolded with a chuckle. He leaned forward, one hand still curled around his cup, the

71

other free to take up her hand again. He studied her with curiosity.

"If you don't think I'll be intruding, I'd like to come to dinner."

She smiled shyly. "Now, my only problem is how to introduce you to my dad."

"Try something novel," he suggested with a mocking grin. "Tell him my name's Colby Sherman, and I'm a lieutenant with the local Gestapo."

"I'll do that, and then I'll leave you to his tender mercies," she threatened, and they both laughed. "The fact is that my neighbor reported seeing me leaving the house with you yesterday, and my father was very curious about you."

"Are you asking me to dinner to pacify your father?" he inquired with a note of challenge in his voice.

Was she? Lauren drew her brows together, trying to decide just what had made her ask him to dinner when she already had a full house to worry about. *You like him, and you want to see him all you can, that's why!*

"Actually, I asked you because I enjoy your company. Is that all right?"

It was more than all right. Colby smiled with satisfaction. "Where I come from, out in the boonies of southwestern Texas, when a man is invited to dinner, he brings the hostess a gift. What can I bring for you?"

Lauren pretended to give it thoughtful consideration and pertly remarked, "A genie who'll do the cleanup after dinner."

"I don't fit into any lamp, but will I do?"

"You don't know what you're letting yourself in for!" She laughed, and after a moment he joined in her laughter.

Later, as they were driving home, Colby reminded her about the invitation. "I was serious when I asked what you'd like me to bring. If you'll tell me what you're serving, perhaps I can supply the wine?"

"Thank you, but no. I've got everything under control."
Well, maybe not everything. She flashed him a nervous
smile. "As families go, mine's pretty special to me, but—"

With a laugh in his voice Colby interrupted. "But they'll
be curious to know how we met, and you don't want them to
know about the crank caller."

"That's about the size of it."

"Leave everything to me. By the time you serve dessert, I
will have passed muster without breathing a word about
how we met."

"I'll tell them eventually about the caller," she explained.
"It's just that if I were to tell them now, my dad would
worry . . . to the point of canceling his vacation." With a
short laugh she added, "Knowing him, he'd probably move
in with me just to make sure I was safe."

His tone half serious, half teasing, Colby suggested, "I
could promise to keep a vigil."

Lauren laughed softly. He had sounded a bit too eager. "I
really think my best bet is not to tell him about the caller
until after it's all over."

"Well, you can't say I didn't offer."

No. No, she couldn't. Lauren studied Colby's strong
hands as they moved over the wheel, her thoughts slowly
wandering over the memory of his kiss earlier that evening.
Suddenly she shivered.

"Cold?"

Lauren looked at him with wide, blank eyes.

"There's a blanket behind your seat," Colby said as he
reached behind them. "Ahh . . ." He brought out the blanket and draped it across her upper body while Lauren
watched him in amused silence.

"Thank you." There was no sense in telling him that she
wasn't cold.

A warm, comfortable silence settled between them as the
shiny black car sped toward her home.

CHAPTER FIVE

I hope she'll ask me in for a nightcap, Colby thought as he helped Lauren from the car. Once inside, he would allow nature to take its course. He wanted her. All through dinner and the ride home the idea of making love with her had sweetly meandered through his thoughts. And now it was more than a wish; it had become a burning need.

His hand felt hot; its heat radiated up her arm and seemed to flow through her entire body. Lauren squeezed her eyes shut against a funny, disturbing, fiery sensation that spread across her lower abdomen. She understood what was happening. She knew what it felt like to want a man. But it had never been like this. No, never like this.

But you're not going to do anything about it, she told herself sternly. She'd never gone in for one-night stands, and she wasn't about to start now. She sneaked a look at Colby through her lashes and inwardly sighed with regret. No, not even for someone like him, who had kept her pulses jumping all night with every look, every touch, every smile.

"Thank you," she whispered, and slipped her hand from his.

His response was to bend down and touch his mouth to hers in the lightest of kisses. Caught by surprise, Lauren sucked in her breath. Noisily, as it turned out. Which made him laugh.

"I guess I should've settled for the more conventional 'You're welcome,' huh?" he teased.

Oh, Lord! Lauren's mind raced for some quick, smart-alecky retort and went blank. Feeling like the village idiot, she stood there, staring up at him, her eyes large in silent appeal.

"On the other hand," he murmured, "this is better." Slipping his hands under her elbows, he brought her up to meet his mouth in a kiss that was a deliberate attempt to rob her of the last bit of wits she had left. His mouth moved with unbelievable tenderness across hers, teasing, seducing all her senses, arousing her to a hunger she had never experienced before.

Lauren slowly wound her arms around his neck; her fingers weaved their way through his flaxen hair; and her body strained against his, seeking a closer intimacy.

Her movements nearly were Colby's undoing. And his body temperature shot up with the urgency of wanting her.

His whispered "Oh, Lauren," was like the soft caress of a light spring breeze blowing over her naked skin. His arms drew her to him, tightening to mold her slender form to the hard firmness of his. His mouth came down again, deftly coaxing hers to open to him. At first tentative, explorative, the thrust of his tongue soon became commanding, driving her to a deeper hunger, an overwhelming need.

Lauren was on the brink of casting off her earlier resolve when the soft, sensuous silence that surrounded them was rent by a piercing scream. Colby stiffened in Lauren's arms.

It was a strange phenomenon, Lauren thought. He hadn't moved an inch, but for all intents and purposes Colby Sherman had abandoned her. He stood with his arms draped loosely around her, his head stiffly erect, his eyes narrowed as he tried to pinpoint the location of the scream.

I guess you can take the badge away from the cop, but you can't take the cop away from the badge, Lauren told herself, her mouth curling with a cynical smile.

In this part of town a scream in the night was not that unusual. The folks on the next block were always feuding over one thing or another. But as long as Colby was so preoccupied, she would consider it a godsend and retreat with her dignity intact. Very carefully, she slipped out of his arms.

While she was rummaging through her bag for her key, she heard a female voice yelling at someone to keep the noise down. A male voice responded with a shouted obscenity that resounded mockingly through the air, and then the night reclaimed its soothing silence.

"This is some neighborhood you live in," Colby grumbled, bringing his attention back down to her.

Lauren grinned. "I happen to like it. A lot."

Scowling, he declared, "We get two, three calls a week from that street."

"You can't say the same thing about my street, though." She gave a dry laugh. "And you can't put my call in the same category."

"That's right." There was a strange quality in his deep voice, and in the eyes that were suddenly too intent on her mouth.

Lauren's mouth went dry. And despite the crisp night air that fanned her face, she felt too warm. Every nerve end tingled with warning; she couldn't afford to get involved with a man who wasn't free to give her what she wanted and needed from a relationship.

"I'd ask you in for a drink, but I'm really bushed. That darned ball game took more out of me than I realized." Her eyes looked right into his as she smiled. "Thanks for a wonderful evening."

When a cynical half-smile crooked one corner of his mouth, Lauren realized that she had been found out. "I have the perfect cure for those aching, tired muscles," Colby said, his tone at once suggestive and amused. His arms went around her, locking her in a tight embrace. She couldn't resist looking up. His smile was still teasing in quality, but it was his eyes that disturbed her. The look that darkened them aroused a welter of emotions, some that frightened her, some that puzzled her. Those that scared her far outweighed the others, and she felt an explosive need to push him away.

Her voice sounding far more stable than it had a right to be, she started, "I think this is where the lady says goodnight and the gentleman goes home—"

"To a cold shower," he finished for her, forcing both a smile and a lightness to his voice.

"That's not what I was going to say." She licked her lips nervously. "But if it's appropriate . . ." She shrugged.

"More than appropriate." He chuckled without mirth. "Necessary." He lowered his arms away from her and stepped back, stretching a hand to her. "If you'll give me your key, I'll go in and check out your house before I go home to that cold shower."

Looking down in embarrassment, Lauren automatically dropped her key into his palm. She was surprised that he could be so sweet to her when she had obviously disappointed him.

He opened the door, and before he'd even crossed the threshold he flipped on the switch that spread light not only over the foyer in which he stood but also the combination office–living room. Everything looked as it had earlier. Walking on into the living room, he was conscious of Lauren treading carefully behind him, and he grinned, recalling those old Charlie Chan shows in which Number One Son's black companion crept cautiously behind the adventuresome young man.

Lauren had to admit that she felt slightly guilty as he left her and hurried through the house, making certain that no one had violated her privacy during her absence.

I'm a fourteen-carat idiot for sending you away, she thought, her expression going mournful as she watched Colby walking back to her.

"All's well," he said. He'd made a quick search of the entire house, paying particular attention that the windows were closed and locked, and the two back exits secured. He smiled with satisfaction as he glanced around him and noticed that the broken window had been fixed.

"Thank you for checking things out for me."

He nodded. "Goes with the badge."

The edge in his voice, underscoring the flicker of annoyance in his eyes, made Lauren uneasy. "Above and beyond the call of duty," she countered in a soft whisper.

"Actually, no." His tone was smooth, his smile easy. "It was my pleasure," he went on. "I needed to know you'd be safe before I could leave you. Speaking of which . . ." As relaxed as the smile on his face was the arm that went around her shoulders to draw her to him.

Lauren tipped her face up, her eyes beseeching him to stop. She had a horrible dread that the next kiss would be the one to break down all the barriers. She couldn't handle a one-sided love affair, simply couldn't. There were too many women in Colby's life. She couldn't, wouldn't, allow herself to become one of many. She made a halfhearted attempt to pull away, but he didn't let go.

"Just one kiss, Lauren," he murmured. "What harm can there be in a little good-night kiss?"

Plenty! a frantic little voice screamed inside her head. But it was too late. As if mesmerized, Lauren watched as his head slowly bent toward her, and then her eyes could see nothing but his hooded eyes, his lips parted in smile. His lips ignited her with a sweet hot flame that engulfed her until there was no reality but that of the strong arms that held her, and the gentle mastery of the tongue that coaxed its way into her mouth.

Finally he pulled away. He stood for a moment looking down at her, and then, as though he had just become aware of it, he lifted a finger to the crazy pulse that was jerking violently at the base of her throat. "It's late," he murmured, smiling into her eyes, "and this hardworking lieutenant should be in bed." She had the distinct impression he was not thinking of *his* bed.

"Thank you again for dinner, and for making certain that my house was safe."

Accepting temporary defeat, Colby let his arms drop to his sides and took a step back. He drew in a deep breath, as if he'd been too long deprived of oxygen. "Good night, Lauren," he whispered, and turned to go.

"Good night, Col—" Her words were rudely interrupted by the ringing of the phone. Stiffening instantly, she lifted frightened eyes to Colby's face.

"You have nothing to fear," he said soothingly. "I'm here. Nothing can hurt you." Warm with reassurance his fingers curled around her wrist to lead her to the phone. His other hand clamped down over the phone, lifted it to her ear, and then he bent toward her, pressing his cheek against hers to listen with her.

Her eyes grew helplessly moist when a disgustingly familiar voice taunted, "It's about time you got home, dear Laurie." Instinctively, she reached down to slam the receiver home, but Colby's hand stopped her. He made a rolling signal with his hand to let her know he wanted her to keep the caller talking.

She didn't have to encourage him. "Where've you been?" the raspy voice demanded. "I've been calling and calling, wondering where you were." When he paused, Lauren breathed a sigh of relief. But her relief was short lived. The man was not through harassing her. "Who were you with, Laurie?" he taunted. "And what were you doing with him, huh?"

Struggling against losing control, Lauren channeled the force of her concentration to the man beside her. She allowed herself to relish the warmth of his body, the tensile strength in the arm that surrounded her, the feel of his skin as his cheek moved slightly against hers.

When she finally spoke, she managed to sound almost bored. "All right, creep, what do you want this time?"

A harsh, grating laugh assaulted her senses. "You know what I want, baby." There was a brief pause, and then, "Or have you been giving it away again?" the voice drawled hatefully.

Lauren's mouth rounded into an *"Oh"* of chagrin, and she started down with the receiver; but Colby stopped her. With hand signals he instructed her to keep the caller on the line. And while she was being verbally abused, he was reaching into her desk for pen and paper. He quickly scribbled on the pad and then held it out for her to read.

Tell him you want to meet him, he'd written.

"Are you insane?" she hissed, her eyes literally shooting off sparks. She gave a violent shake of her head. For goodness' sakes, she wanted to be rid of the scum, not make a phone mate of him! What could he be thinking to suggest she do such an asinine thing?

Colby stared at her for a moment, then raised his eyes to the ceiling in exasperation. He understood her reaction, sympathized with her feelings, but this was something that needed to be done. When he opened his eyes again, he smiled to reassure her, and soundlessly mouthed, "Trust me!" Directing her attention to the pad, he wrote: *Try to make your voice sound friendly, sexy.*

Sexy? Lauren tried to scream the word, but it stuck in her throat. Anger surged through her, anger that was equally attributable to the vermin on the phone and the man who was forcing her to endure this outrage. When finally she spoke, her voice was sensually husky because of the knot of exasperation that seemed to be lodged in her throat. "I'd like to meet you," she said.

"Bravo!" Colby whispered. When he tried to put his arm around her again, she flung him away and spun out of his reach.

He followed her, his arrogant jaw jutting out with determination. He rested his elbow on her shoulder and held the notepad in front of her eyes.

Ask him to come to you, Lauren read.

She pulled in a deep, restorative breath, wrested the pen from him, and wrote, *Like hell I will!* Her chin was lifted in obstinacy. She'd have to have one foot inside the laughing academy before she'd ask that garbage to her home!

"Where can we meet?" she asked. "And when?" Even to her ears her voice sounded blatantly insincere.

Silence.

Lauren nearly sagged, but whether with relief because she had stunned the caller into silence or because her knees felt as though they would buckle, she couldn't really tell. Colby seemed to know that she needed him, because he slipped his arms around her and held her close.

"What the hell kind of trap are you trying to lure me into, bitch?" the caller demanded viciously.

Lauren felt Colby stiffen, and she heard his sharp intake of breath. Her hand tightened around the phone until her knuckles went white, and she achieved a modicum of calm. "Why would I want to set a trap for you?" she asked, her voice marvelously cool and calm.

"Because you think you can outsmart me. But you can't, Laurie. I'm far too clever for you." An ugly, mocking laugh preceded the sudden hum that told her he had hung up on her.

Colby swore harshly and stepped away from her, scowling. Lauren hastily dropped the phone and turned to face him.

Colby saw the lines of worry that stretched across her brow, the hurt and angry look in her eyes, and his heart went out to her. Suddenly, he wanted only to hold her until the anger and hurt melted away from her body. But he knew he couldn't, shouldn't.

Applying mental brakes to his sympathetic urges, he smiled briefly. "I don't think you'll be bothered again tonight, but if you are, I want you to call me immediately." Taking one of his business cards, he wrote his personal number on the back of it and laid the card down beside the phone.

"Why did you do all that?" she forced through gritted teeth.

Colby didn't even pretend not to understand what she was asking. "I wanted to shake him up a little, call his bluff."

Surprise briefly sparked in her eyes. "And suppose that he had decided to come? What then?" She fixed him with an icy stare.

"He wouldn't have come."

"You don't know that."

He shifted impatiently. "I'm a cop, Lauren. I've dealt with his kind before."

She was still staring at him angrily.

"Dammit, Lauren. I wouldn't have told you to encourage him if I thought you'd be in any danger. I don't work that way."

"Neither do I," she flung back at him, the last shreds of her control slipping away. "And I don't appreciate being put in such a precarious position. What the hell kind of cop are you, anyway, that you have to use me in order to do your job? A job, I might add, that my taxes pay for!"

For a millisecond he looked like a man who's been dealt a severe blow without warning. His eyes widened, narrowed, darkened. If she were any other citizen, he might have been tempted to walk out on her. Hers was only one of a dozen cases requiring immediate attention. Not necessarily his personal attention.

But he knew he couldn't go. He ran impatient fingers through his wind-tossed hair. "You want him caught, don't you?" he challenged with a contained force that startled her.

"Yes!" she shouted. "But, dammit, Colby, I don't relish being the cheese on your damned trap!" She felt vulnerable, and she didn't like it.

Jamming his hands in his pockets, Colby studied her in moody silence and took note of the angry flush that stained her cheeks, and the light of battle that gleamed in her eyes. Yielding to a sudden, purely masculine impulse, he lifted his hands to her shoulders and very gently drew her to him. She was trembling.

"I'm not going to let anything happen to you, Lauren," he promised in a soft, soothing murmur. His arms went around her slowly, and he held her to him, his hands lightly, warmly, stroking her back until her trembling had subsided.

At last, he gently set her away. "Would you like me to stay with you for a little while?" he asked softly. "At least until you fall asleep?"

Lauren shook her head. "Thank you, but I'll be all right now." There was no sense in his staying any longer. She had a dreadful feeling that she might never sleep again, anyway.

"Are you sure?"

"Positive," she said with false bravado as she led the way to the door.

After Colby had left, and she had secured the deadbolt in place, Lauren switched off the lights and went into her bedroom, feeling vaguely tearful.

A couple of aspirin helped to ease her nervousness, but she slept only fitfully, often waking during the night with her heart pounding in panic for no explicable reason. There were no nightmares. No, not even dreams.

Finally at five, she gave up all pretense of sleeping and left her bed feeling limp and irritable.

While the coffee was brewing, she showered and dressed in faded jeans and a sloppy T-shirt, her "uniform" for housekeeping chores. She pulled her hair back with a leather thong, then trod into the kitchen to fix a Spartan breakfast.

Thirty minutes later, as she was enjoying her third cup of coffee, she heard the jangle of the phone. "No," she moaned pitifully, instinctively curling her body into a tight little ball. The cup slipped from her nerveless fingers, spilling its contents and breaking without her even hearing it fall. She felt fragile this morning, unable to cope with any more of the obscene caller's abuse. Squeezing her eyes shut, she instructed her ears to be deaf to the insistent summons of her telephone.

I have nothing to fear, nothing to fear. She repeated the silent litany until it filled her mind and blanked out all outside noise.

Finally, the phone grew silent, but Lauren did not appear to notice. She remained where she was, curled around herself, her forehead resting on her propped-up knees.

A hissing sound coming from somewhere behind her drifted into her ears, and she slowly lifted her head, her eyes searching her surroundings as though they were alien to her. She tracked the hissing to the coffeepot, which she had neglected to unplug. Instantly, she was in motion. And as her feet touched the floor, she noticed the spilled coffee, the broken mug.

"Damn!" exploded from her mouth, followed by a volley of colorful words she seldom used. She ran to the counter, unplugged the coffeepot, and then grabbed the roll of paper towels to clean up her mess. After she'd washed the dishes and left them on the drainer to dry, she took out her cleaning materials and channeled all her energies into making the house presentable for her parents' bon voyage dinner party that evening and for her grandmother's week-long visit.

Lauren was returning the cleaning materials to the cabinet under her kitchen sink when she heard the chime of her doorbell. She froze.

I'm getting paranoid, she thought, one corner of her mouth curving downward with self-disgust. She stood and, dusting her hands on the seat of her jeans, forced herself to walk calmly to the door. For a fleeting instant she felt fear as she eyed the door. And then she released the bolt, wrapped her hand around the knob, and opened the door. She found Colby waiting on the porch.

"I was wondering if your mommy would let you come out and play," he said by way of greeting, grinning adorably, his eyes twinkling with delight.

"My mommy doesn't like me to play with strange men," Lauren teased in return, mimicking his childlike tones.

A smile of pure enjoyment spread over his features, warming the gold of his eyes, creating a disturbance in her breathing. "Actually, I was hoping you'd have lunch with me."

Lauren's gaze swept hastily over his brown suit, immaculate cream-colored shirt, the perfectly knotted brown-striped tie. If she hadn't felt dowdy before, she did then. "I'm not exactly dressed to go out," she said needlessly.

"What if I give you a few minutes to throw on something else?"

"Throw something on?" she repeated, scandalized. "I'll need at least thirty minutes." It would serve him right if she took an hour!

"Make it twenty." He smiled as though unaware that he had ruffled her feathers. "I didn't finish my reports, so I have to go back to them after a quick lunch."

She took forty minutes just to be perverse.

Once in Colby's snazzy Porsche, they headed toward a smorgasbord in the next town. There, over a delicious variety of Oriental dishes, they talked about their day and briefly touched on the evening's dinner menu.

"I tried to call you from the station, but you didn't answer your phone."

"I was indisposed," she lied, and thrust out her chin in a way that amused him.

His laugh resounded tauntingly around the room, turning several heads in their direction. "I suspected you just weren't answering your phone today."

"It's not that funny!" He was having too much fun at her expense. Her eyes glinted mutinously as they were lifted to his smiling face. "I wonder how you'd react if our positions were reversed."

"You're angry with me," he teased in a drawling voice.

The amusement lurking in his eyes was contagious. Lauren couldn't resist laughing. "I don't understand why, but you seem to bring out the worst in me."

One corner of his mouth lifted in a lopsided grin, and his eyes brightened with glee. "Must be because you bring out the devil in me."

Their eyes met, locked. Lauren felt the spark, deep and electrifying, that always flared up between them. Slowly, his hand stretched toward hers. A deep, rapid flow of exhilaration rushed through her as his fingers curled around her hand.

"You're very beautiful, Lauren, you know that?" he said quietly, his eyes straying away from hers to wander over her tawny features, almost tangibly tracing the line of her small nose, the soft, coral-tinged mouth that had opened like a flower to the sun under his mouth the night before. He had only to close his eyes to relive that pleasurable memory.

"I owe it all to my grandfather's good taste," she said with an embarrassed laugh. It had never been easy for her to accept a compliment. "He threw over an ebony-eyed Spaniard to marry my Finnish grandmother, whom I resemble."

"Good for Grandpa." Entranced, he continued to study her, his gaze sweeping over her loosely arranged blond hair and delicate features.

Lauren began to feel unusually warm under his unwavering scrutiny. She gave a nervous tug on her hand, and he released it. She quickly lowered it to her lap, clasping it with her other hand as though afraid it would reach out of its own volition to join with his again. At that gesture his lips parted in a grin that increased her discomfort.

Her chin went up a fraction. "Isn't it about time you got back to your paperwork?"

His eyes widened. "You wouldn't be trying to get rid of me, would you?" He laughed, a full, rich baritone that irritated her because he was mocking her again.

"Not in the least," she countered smoothly. "It's just that you have paperwork waiting for you, and I have to go to the grocery store."

"Why don't I help you with the shopping after I finish with my paperwork?" His voice was a low murmur as he ran his fingers thoughtfully around the rim of his coffee cup. "You know what they say, two heads are better than one," he added with a wink, his gaze moving caressingly over her face.

She was disappointed he had not suggested they do her shopping first, but she refused to let it show in her voice. She smiled. "'They' are always saying things like that, but in this instance I think that we'll both be better off if I do the shopping and you return to your own work."

"Heartless woman," he accused in a low, playful murmur. He got up quickly and then helped her out of her chair. For a tingling moment his hand rested on her waist, and his breath warmly brushed the top of her ear.

When they parted twenty minutes later, Lauren felt disappointed yet oddly relieved. She had too many things to do and didn't need the sort of distraction that Colby Sherman provided. With such little effort, too, she amended, laughing softly.

CHAPTER SIX

Long after her parents had departed, Lauren stood in the kitchen looking out the window, wishing she could shake off her blue mood. Ever since Colby had called to apologize because he would be unable to join her for dinner, she had felt vaguely despondent. Oh, she had put on a happy face for her family's sake, but it had been a strain, and she had been very relieved to see them go.

"Would you like me to help you with the dishes, dear?" her grandmother asked.

Lauren turned and smiled as she shook her head. "What I should've done was ask Jill and Donnie to do them."

Catherine Shayler gave a slight toss of her head and wrinkled her small nose. "They probably wouldn't have left one single dish intact." She uttered a sound that was a cross between a laugh and a hiccup. "Oh, my," she exclaimed, lifting a dainty hand to her mouth. "I think you gave me too much to drink tonight."

"*I* gave you too much to drink?" Lauren shot back, eyes wide with disbelief. "Who was the one who kept holding out her glass each time the bottle went around?"

Her grandmother's green eyes gleamed with amusement. "I couldn't be impolite and not celebrate having your father gone for a couple of weeks, now could I?"

"Grandmother!"

Catherine chuckled, thoroughly enjoying her granddaughter's discomfort. "Now, be honest, Laurie," she prompted.

"Tell me you're not going to enjoy having him a few thousand miles away for a few days?" Her look was direct, challenging, and very much amused.

With a sheepish grin Lauren admitted, "Well, it will be nice to have him out of my hair for a few days."

"My sentiments exactly!" Sliding the sleeves of her blue silk dress up to her elbows, Catherine moved determinedly toward the sink. But Lauren got there first.

"You're my guest." She gave her grandmother's slight shoulders a loving squeeze and then playfully shoved her aside. "Shoo! Go find something to read, or just go into the living room and vegetate."

"I'll have time enough later on to, as you so quaintly put it, vegetate. And until I have to, I will make myself useful." She gave Lauren a not-too-gentle elbow jab in the ribs. "You go on. Take your shower, do your nails, or whatever it is you do at this time of night, and leave me to do the dishes in peace."

"Aye, aye, Cap'n Bligh!" Lauren saluted her smartly and then sidestepped in an attempt to avoid a swat on the behind. She wasn't fast enough. The soft black knit of her pantsuit beautifully molded her nicely rounded buttocks, but it was no buffer against the power behind the slap. Her skin was left tingling.

"For a shortie, you sure pack a mean wallop," Lauren grumbled, rubbing the abused spot. Her grandmother was unremorseful.

"If you're determined to make a pest of yourself, you may as well help. Get a towel and dry these dishes."

"I've got a great idea, Gram," Lauren said, her eyes bright with amusement, but her expression faultlessly innocent. "Why don't I dry the dishes?"

"Brat!" Catherine shook her head in mock despair and then chuckled.

"If I am, it's because you spoiled me rotten while I was growing up," Lauren teased. She draped the towel across her shoulder and undid the tie of her wraparound bodice, hastily reaching inside to scratch along her waistline. She had tied the bands too tightly. "I think I ate too much," she complained, gently running her nails over the faint ridges and light indentations the band had left on her skin.

"Too much?" Catherine countered, critically eyeing her granddaughter's slim figure. "You don't eat enough to keep a sparrow from starving," she went on, huffily.

An old and very sore subject that Lauren was determined to avoid at all costs was her dietary habits. "Did you notice how big Donnie is getting?" she said, and realized immediately she had given her grandmother an opening to take another potshot at her.

"That's because he eats right and drinks plenty of milk."

"If I ate the way he does, I'd be the summer replacement for the Goodyear blimp, thank you.

"Anyway, at the rate that boy's growing, he'll probably be as tall as Rob, don't you think?" Although he'd never be as cute. . . .

Catherine nodded, and as she squirted detergent into the dishpan, she murmured, "I just hope he'll grow up to be as strong too."

A shiver of apprehension slithered up Lauren's spine. She understood what her grandmother was hinting. "Tell me about Eleanor, Gram," she whispered, feeling almost as if she ought to check over her shoulder to assure herself that Donnie and Jill were not within hearing distance. No one ever spoke of Eleanor, and until tonight Lauren hadn't had such a perfect opportunity to satisfy her curiosity. "You knew them both before Rob married her, didn't you?"

Catherine nodded. "She was a weak, self-indulgent woman, but she was beautiful," Catherine said. There was a spiteful edge to her voice. "She was accustomed to having everything her way. She should never have married Robert." She gave an angry swipe at a stubborn spot on a glass, then dipped the glass into the rinse water and handed it to Lauren.

"Robert was young, idealistic, ambitious. He needed a wife who was supportive, understanding." As she handed Lauren another glass, she added, "Something that Eleanor was definitely not!"

No, she was not. Lauren had been only thirteen when Donnie was born, but she could remember how bitterly Eleanor complained because he was born with a stomach disorder. She knew now that all parents with babies in the house complain about sleepless nights, colicky bouts, astronomical utility and food bills, and disrupted social lives. But even then, she had sensed that to Eleanor, the second baby was an inconvenience.

Sympathy for baby Donnie surged through her, and for a few minutes she forgot what a brat he could be at times.

"Very soon after Donnie was born, Eleanor started to drink, to carry on with men she picked up at the bars where she spent all her time." Catherine paused, and for the longest time she stared at the plate she had just washed.

"Poor little things," she murmured, her normally soft voice husky with emotion. "She would lock them in Jilly's bedroom with a box of cereal and a bottle of milk for each of them. Jill was too little to take care of herself, let alone look after her baby brother. Poor little thing," Catherine murmured again, almost to herself.

"How long did she carry on like that?" Lauren felt a murderous rage toward Eleanor for having been so uncaring.

"Too long," her grandmother grumbled. "She was a devil, that one. She would do her running around while Robert was at work, but when he came home, she'd meet him at the door, complaining that she hadn't gotten the house clean, or picked up his laundry, or done the groceries, because the children had been little hellions all day long."

"And, of course, Rob believed her."

Catherine nodded. "He had no reason not to. By the time

91

he came home, it was late, and the children would be sound asleep. Besides, they were too young to contradict whatever Eleanor decided to tell him.

"And then one day he saw her leaving a bar with one of her lovers. They were so drunk, they had to hold each other up as they stumbled toward her car. Robert said that he was tempted to follow them, to confront her, to drag her back home if necessary. But then he reconsidered and decided it was best if he went home to his children for the time being."

"And, of course, he found them alone, right?"

Catherine sighed. "She'd left them alone again. It was a good thing that Robert decided to come home. Jilly had somehow managed to get out of the bedroom through a window and had fallen into the pool."

"Oh, my word!"

Her grandmother smiled thinly. "He got there just in time to prevent her from drowning."

They were finished with the dishes. Lauren draped the sodden towel over the handle of the oven door, then took the tube of moisturizing lotion she kept on the sink counter and squeezed a generous amount into her hand.

"Want some?"

"Thank you, dear." Smiling, Catherine held out her hands.

"So what did Rob do then?"

Smoothing the rich emollient over her hands, Catherine continued with some reluctance. "He was mad enough to kill Eleanor for leaving his babies alone, but he was more concerned over his daughter. He bundled the children into the car and went to have Jill checked by the family physician.

"Eleanor never came home that day. And that night, after Robert had fed and put the children to bed, a policeman came to tell him that she had been seriously injured in a car accident and had been taken to a nearby hospital. Robert asked your mother to come stay with the babies, and rushed to the hospital. Poor man, he was too late. Eleanor was dead."

"How is it that there was no scandal over how she died?" Lauren frowned. She remembered that all the local papers had carried news of her death, but all they'd reported was that the accident had occurred along Niles Canyon and was blamed on faulty brakes.

"Robert managed somehow to avoid it."

"And he's never told the children the truth about her," Lauren remarked softly.

By this time they were in the living room. Catherine slowly lowered herself onto the couch and lifted her legs up, throwing an afghan she had brought with her over them. As she fixed the decorative pillows behind her, she said, "That is why they're so resentful of your sister. They were babies when their mother died, so they know only what Robert has told them about her. Poor man, he wanted only to make them feel loved by her, but he went overboard and now they're convinced that she was a wonderful mother. They resent Jeanne's attempts to love them because they're convinced she's trying to take Eleanor's place in their hearts."

"Jeanne tries too hard," Lauren said, and suddenly all the resentment she felt against the two Hunter children resurfaced. "If I were in her shoes, I'd—"

"You'd do no such thing," Catherine snapped. "In fact, you would work every bit as hard as Jeanne is doing to get them back on the right track."

"Maybe," Lauren conceded ungraciously. "But I wouldn't put up with all the things Jeanne does."

There was loving indulgence in Catherine's eyes and smile. "It's a funny fact of life that we can't understand the other fellow's attitude until we're forced to stand in his shoes."

It was her way of saying that Lauren was being too judgmental. "I guess you're right," Lauren admitted with an embarrassed smile as she went to the sofa, to perch herself on the armrest facing her grandmother. "But it's very hard to see Jeanne bending over backward in an effort to please those little brats when they will never appreciate her."

"Oh, they'll come around," Catherine promised with the confidence of twenty years of teaching in public schools and the experience earned in raising four active, demanding, and very independent children of her own.

"I hope so, for Jeanne's sake." Lauren bent down and took off her sandals, with a sigh of great relief dropping them onto the floor. She burrowed her stockinged feet under the afghan and mischievously tickled her grandmother's feet, laughing when Catherine drew her legs up and out of her way.

"It's a little bit late for visitors, isn't it?" Catherine asked when a knock sounded on the front door.

"A bit." Jumping from her perch, Lauren padded across the room to the door, her heart beating erratically with a mingling of apprehension and anticipation. She hoped Colby had decided to come visit, and at the same time she was afraid that some form of danger awaited her on the other side of the door.

"Who is it?" she demanded with false bravado. She flashed a glance over her shoulder at Catherine. Whatever it took, she must not allow her grandmother to see that she was afraid.

"Open the door, Laurie."

Slurred, but undeniably Colby's voice. Caught between smiling because it was he, and frowning because she strongly suspected he'd been drinking, Lauren cautiously opened the door just a crack. She wouldn't want her grandmother to meet him for the first time when he was not at his best.

"Hi," she said, her smile huge and as friendly as she could make it under the circumstances.

"Hi, yershelf," he returned, going back on his heels. "Yer both verry beautiful," he added, laughing.

Both? Since he couldn't see her grandmother from the

porch, he had to be seeing double. Great! Lauren thought grumpily.

"Been having fun, have we?"

Colby wasn't so drunk he couldn't detect the sarcasm in her voice. His strong white teeth flashed in the darkness as he grinned. "Mished you, though," he admitted, and without warning his arm snaked around her waist and drew her to him. Lauren released the door and quickly held up both her hands to ward him off.

"It's late," she said, desperately holding on to her temper. "We both have to go to work tomorrow." Her hands were now pressed against his chest, and she was fighting against acknowledging the sensual feel of the silk shirt that stretched across his broad chest, the warmth of the skin beneath it, and the strong, steady beat of his heart.

"S'not zo late," he argued, firming his hold on her. He seemed to lurch toward her, and instinctively, Lauren pulled back. He did not release her.

"You're drunk!" she hissed, and cringed when he started laughing.

"Jest a l'il bit." He lifted his free hand and tried to give her a hint as to how little he had drunk, using his index finger and thumb. The problem was that he couldn't keep any space between them, and it amused him so, he started laughing again.

Wanting only to silence him, Lauren rushed a hand up to cover his mouth. A mistake, as she was soon to discover. A shiver overwhelmed her when the fiend caressed the center of her palm with the tip of his tongue. As though she had been burned, Lauren pulled her hand away and stood staring up at him, breathing rapidly, her face flushed.

"I don't mean to intrude, Laurie," her grandmother said from directly behind her. "I just wanted to tell you goodnight."

Cold water could not have sobered Colby any faster than Catherine's sudden appearance. If she hadn't been so embarrassed, Lauren might have laughed at his dumbfounded expression.

She turned partway toward her grandmother and, faltering, made the introductions.

Catherine's smile was sweet, amused, and indulgent. She held out her hand, saying, "It's a pleasure to meet you, Colby."

"The pleashure's mine," Colby said, taking her hand, losing it between both of his. Although his voice was still slightly slurred, he was very charming and delighted Catherine by telling her the resemblance between her and Lauren was unmistakable.

"You really think so?" Catherine remarked, easing her hand from his hold. She reached up and casually patted her silvery-gray hair. It was short, feathered around her face to flatter her still youthful features.

"Cross m'heart," Colby averred, lifting a hand to his chest, standing at attention as though he were saluting the flag.

Nodding with understanding, Catherine turned to smile at Lauren. "Why don't I go into the kitchen and start the coffee for you, dear?" She patted Lauren's arm and then whisked herself away before either Lauren or Colby could respond.

"Coffee?" he repeated, arching his eyebrows.

"Black and strong, and hopefully acrid."

His grin was crooked, amused. "D'you really think I need it?"

"Desperately!"

"Only one thing I need desperately," he contradicted in a low murmur, drawing her into his arms before Lauren could even think to prevent it.

Where was her grandmother when she needed her? Lauren wondered grumpily when she felt herself being literally lifted off her feet and carried out onto the porch.

"This isn't funny!"

"It's the most fun I've had all evening!" His breath fanned her face, warm and whiskey-flavored.

Lauren looked up at him and frowned fiercely. "I had the impression earlier that you were looking forward to going to dinner with the mayor." She made a passable effort to free herself and realized the futility of it. His arms were much too strong, and he was outrageously determined to thwart her every effort.

"It was all right, but I would've much rather been with you."

She smiled. "That's nice."

He pressed a kiss on the tip of her nose, then pulled back and looked into her eyes for a long time before he spoke again. "I keep telling you that I'm nice, but you keep needing to be convinced." Laughing huskily, he tightened his arms around her, and then his mouth was on hers, soft, coaxing, teasing.

"A lot of convincing," Lauren murmured, slipping her arms between them, curling them around his strong neck.

She thought she heard him groan as she moved against him, and then he shifted restlessly, clinging to her as he relaxed against the porch wall. His lips brushed her temple, gently closed her eyes, nibbled at the sensitive corners of her mouth, probing until she opened her mouth to his.

Perched precariously on the edge of throwing caution to the winds and inviting him to make love to her, Lauren picked up the sounds of her grandmother's quick steps coming toward them and reluctantly pushed out of Colby's delicious embrace.

Colby had heard Catherine's footsteps also and allowed Lauren to escape. He was breathing rapidly, the pulse at his throat echoing the erratic beat of his heart.

"Saved by Grandma," he mocked out of the corner of his mouth.

"And none too soon," Lauren added shakily, trembling with awareness even as she stepped away from him. She shivered as though with cold and rubbed her arms, disturbingly aware that he was watching her every move.

"Would you like a cup of coffee?" She turned toward the door, almost wishing that he would say he had to hurry home. She was too vulnerable to him just now, too conscious of his sensuality, to want him in the same room with her while her grandmother was present.

"I wouldn't want to disappoint your grandmother," he said.

He hadn't disappointed Catherine. "He's one of the nicest men you've ever introduced to me," she said as Lauren came back to her after having seen Colby to the door.

"I'm glad you like him," Lauren said, smiling.

"He's right for you."

Lauren stared, nearly gaping. "One brief meeting, and you're already fixing me up for life with him?"

Catherine smiled confidently. "Only because I had the advantage of watching you both when you thought I wasn't looking. He loves you, Laurie." Catherine beamed, and Lauren had a hunch that in her mind, her grandmother was already visualizing a big church wedding for her and Colby.

"Don't rush out to buy the rice, Gram," Lauren cautioned with a laugh. "You know my track record."

Catherine shook her head. "You won't get cold feet with this one," she assured her. "Those other times, you knew deep down in your heart that those boys were not for you."

"There were only two, Grandmother," Lauren defended. "Please don't make it sound like I've had hordes of them literally knocking down my door to propose to me."

"They were boys, Laurie. Colby Sherman is a man."

She couldn't, wouldn't, argue with that. Lauren grinned. "And what a man!" she declared saucily, and, grabbing an astonished Catherine, waltzed with her into the kitchen.

"Silly child!" Catherine declared, laughing delightedly as

she escaped Lauren's hands. "It's no wonder your poor father despairs of you growing up."

"Oh, pooh! Daddy would worry just for the sake of worrying," Lauren countered, laughing softly. "His problem is that he doesn't want me to stop being his 'little girl.' I swear! I'll be in my dotage, and he'll still think he has to take care of me."

"Marry Colby and that will stop," Catherine suggested. "I have a hunch that Matthew would think twice before he tried to run roughshod over you if you had Colby around."

"Great!" Lauren laughed dryly. "I can't think of a worse reason for marrying a guy."

Catherine mischievously enumerated several reasons that were far worse and, laughing at Lauren's appalled expression, said good-night and left the room.

"Now I know where I get my outrageously bad sense of humor," Lauren whispered under her breath, her eyes gleaming with repressed amusement as they watched her grandmother moving away.

Slipping down on the sofa, she gathered the afghan around her. Sundays were her days to catch up with her reading. She was a sucker for the children who canvassed the neighborhood for various selling campaigns, and consequently received more magazines than she would ever read.

But she had her favorites, and she would always make time for them. As she settled back against the cushions, she began to leaf through the latest Ellery Queen. But she couldn't concentrate on the written page. Her thoughts kept darting back to Colby.

Hugging the magazine to her chest, she closed her eyes and allowed her mind to recall those few minutes with Colby outside on the porch.

Was her grandmother right about him? Was he pursuing her because he cared for her, or was she just another in a long line of conquests?

A frown broke the smoothness of her brow as she remembered the redheaded waitress at the Dandy Diner.

Then, too, there was Anne Mulrooney.

"Rot!" Flinging the magazine away, she left the couch and went into the kitchen for a glass of warm milk. Only time would tell whether she was being a fool for feeling what she did for Colby Sherman. And she was not going to lose any sleep worrying over it.

CHAPTER SEVEN

Morning came way too soon. Usually grumpy before she had her first cup of coffee, Lauren made a point of dashing out to the kitchen to start a pot of her special brew before her grandmother could get up. It wouldn't do to let Catherine see her in a blue mood again.

While the coffee was perking, she took a quick shower and then curled her hair and dressed in white slacks and a black knit shirt. In deference to her grandmother, who hated to see her barefoot, she slipped into a pair of strappy sandals.

Catherine was in the kitchen, at the stove, when Lauren hurried in for her first cup of coffee.

"No breakfast for me, Gram," she said, stopping long enough to kiss Catherine on the cheek before going to the cupboard to take down a mug. "I usually have only coffee and a piece of toast these days."

"That's why you're just skin and bones" was the sharp rejoinder.

"I am not all skin and bones," Lauren defended quickly, firmly, but her smiling eyes belied her serious expression.

Dressed in a dark-blue robe and matching slippers, with her hair hidden under a frilly night cap, Catherine looked dainty. And frail. But there was nothing in the world that was further from the truth, in Lauren's considered opinion. Her grandmother was forged steel all the way through.

"By the time I send you back home, I'm going to look like

a beached whale," Lauren complained, puffing out her cheeks and opening her eyes as wide as they would go.

"And a week after that, the way you eat, you'll look like a skeleton again," Catherine returned with an amused grin. "Now, go sit down and wait for your breakfast."

With an exaggerated sigh of defeat Lauren took her cup of coffee to the table and sat down to wait.

"How do you want your eggs?"

"Back inside the hen?" Lauren suggested hopefully.

"You'll get them sunny-side up." The warning was issued in a mild voice.

"Heaven forbid! Scramble them, please." She shuddered delicately. There was nothing worse than runny eggs this early in the morning!

After they had breakfasted and Lauren had done the dishes as penance for drowning the eggs in catsup, she went to work, leaving the kitchen free for Catherine to use as she pleased.

Off and on during the morning she was aware of her grandmother's movements in the kitchen. The clanging of pots and pans brought back beautiful memories of her child-hood when she would visit her grandparents in Mendocino and, as usual, her grandmother would cook up a storm.

By noon the house was filled with the most delicious aromas, arousing Lauren's appetite despite herself. She breathed in deeply, teasing her memory to identify the various scents.

"Whatever it is you're cooking, you're making me ravenous!" she called out to her grandmother.

"That's good," Catherine approved. She was walking into the room, in her hands a tray from which emanated the most delicious, mouth-watering smells.

Greedily, Lauren held out her hands, but her grand-mother ignored her and continued walking toward the sofa.

"You go wash up, and everything will be ready when you come back," Catherine said over her shoulder. She set the tray down on the floor, then spread a red linen runner over the coffee table and set up two places with matching napkins, Lauren's best silverware, two wineglasses, and a bottle of dry white wine.

Lauren hurried away, smiling because no matter how old she was, how independent she became, her grandmother simply waltzed into her life and began ordering her around as if she were still in her teens. By the time she returned to the living room, Catherine had already served their lunch.

As they sat around the coffee table, enjoying a delicious variety of Oriental dishes, they discussed Jill and Donnie and the reason that Rob had asked her to baby-sit.

"I'll have to admit that I'm not looking forward to having them both at the same time. And all week too!" Lauren groaned, leaned back on her hands, and stretched her legs out under the table. She felt overfull, although she hadn't even begun to do justice to the generous plate her grandmother had served her.

"They're really no worse than you and your sisters were," Catherine said as she began clearing the table. "Your problem is that you want them to act your age when they're acting theirs." She glanced down at Lauren and softened her scolding with a gentle smile. "You're a bit too intolerant, too impatient. I understand how you feel, though, and I want you to do something with them that will help to make the week a lot easier on you."

Lauren grinned. "Old Pepe's doghouse is still out in the backyard, but I don't think I can stuff both kids into it."

"There were days when I felt like doing that with you and Tish," her grandmother admitted with a faint smile. "Now, back to Jill and Donnie. Take them somewhere for a snack. Maybe an ice cream soda?"

Maybe arsenic on the rocks? With a small, secret smile lurking in her eyes, Lauren lifted herself from the floor in one lithe, fluid movement. "For you, I'll do it," she promised as she whirled around and rushed to answer one of her customers' phones.

After she had passed on the message to the proper party, she went into the kitchen, thinking to help her grandmother with the cleanup. She found Catherine sitting at the table, sipping her wine. Everything in the kitchen was spotless, all the chrome gleaming, shinier than it had been in months.

Smiling, Lauren drew in lungsful of the delicious aroma that permeated the air, holding her breath to savor the smell. "Mmmm, what's in the oven?"

"Cookies. Oatmeal and chocolate chip. The kids really enjoy them."

"No butter cookies?" She made a pouting face.

"Maybe tomorrow."

"I can hardly wait." Feeling pampered, and thoroughly loving it, Lauren returned to the living room and her switchboard.

Frequently during the next couple of hours Lauren's thoughts were on Colby.

She shivered with remembered delight when she thought of the last time she had been in his powerful arms, and recalled the taste of his mouth with such clarity she could almost imagine the flavor of whiskey mingling with her own saliva as she swallowed.

A soft footfall made her turn around, and the lovely fantasy vanished like so much smoke in the air.

"It's two-thirty, dear. Time for you to go get the children," Catherine reminded her.

Lauren nodded. "I have but one life to give to my family," she mumbled, and left her chair. She stood for a couple of minutes rotating her body at the waist to ease the strain from her neck and shoulders.

"The way your back pops, you'd think you were my age," Catherine remarked as she eased herself into Lauren's chair.

"That old I'll never get!" Lauren teased when she was a safe distance away. She wasn't about to give her grand-

mother another opportunity to swat her. "I should be back
—Strike that. I don't know when I'll be back. Maggie should
be here at half past three, and you've handled the phones
before, so I'm not going to worry."

What did worry her was what to do if Jill and Donnie
didn't agree to what her grandmother had suggested they do
together. But as she drove to Donnie's school, she resolved
not to give them the opportunity to refuse her.

She parked her Camaro in front of the school and idly
watched as the students began pouring out the two side
doors and the large front door.

"They all look alike," she whispered, not surprised. Her
mother had said the same thing about her and her peers.

At last she spied Donnie, and without warning she was
flooded with sympathy. He looked bedraggled, with his
dark-red hair sticking out all over, his freckled face smudged
with dirt.

"Oh, Lord, what have you gotten into now?" she wondered out loud just before the boy opened the passenger
door.

"Hi, Donnie."

"Hi." He slid onto the seat, keeping his face downbent.

"Is something wrong?" Frowning, she studied his lean
profile and found a bruise just under his left eye, and a
scratch that ran parallel to his jawline.

"Nothing!" he snapped.

She suspected he'd been fighting. Mulling over what her
grandmother had suggested, she turned the key and started
the engine before turning again to Donnie.

"You look hot and tired." Her voice was soft, marvelously
casual. "How about if we pick Jill up and then go get something to drink?"

"I got homework."

"We won't stay out too long."

"I don't have any money."

Lauren frowned. One of Jeanne's biggest and most frequently voiced complaints was that Rob was too generous with money. She longed to ask what he'd done with the ten dollars she knew Rob gave him every Monday for lunches, but said instead, "Don't worry about it. It'll be my treat."

Donnie slanted her a dubious glance. "What do I have to do for it?"

"Nothing, Donnie."

Disbelief narrowed his light-brown eyes, but he said nothing. And Lauren was glad. She didn't know what she would have said if he had chosen to question her motives further.

She got an almost identical reaction from Jill. But Lauren decided not to let it bother her. At best, the girl had always been indifferent to her.

There was no miraculous sweetening of their feelings toward her, and Lauren hadn't expected there would be, but as they left the car an hour later, she noticed that Donnie's shoulders were not as rigid as they had been earlier. And Jill had even smiled as she thanked her for taking them to the ice-cream parlor, particularly since she had seen her latest heartthrob there.

Maybe there is *something to what Grandma says,* Lauren thought, slinging the strap of her purse over her shoulder preparatory to leaving the car.

When she went into the house, she could hear them in the kitchen with Catherine. They weren't the happy, gregarious children she and her sisters had been, but they responded well to Catherine's loving treatment.

"Oh, I'm glad you're back," Maggie exclaimed, shuffling hastily through a stack of notes on the table.

"Is something wrong?"

"Why do you always think there's something wrong when I say I'm glad you're back?" By this time she'd found what she was looking for, and held the note up with a triumphant, if cheeky, smile. "Colby wants you to call him. Here's his private number."

Lauren's heart hesitated and then started beating, a wild,

joyous hammering. Adopting a passable nonchalant attitude, she took the note from Maggie and slipped it into a pocket of her purse.

"He said it was important," Maggie prompted.

"Well, maybe I *should* call him. . . ." Trying not to hurry, Lauren went to her personal phone and sat down at her desk. Slanting a wary look in Maggie's direction, she was pleased to see that the young girl had returned to work. She quickly dialed.

"Colby Sherman."

"This is Lauren, returning your call." If her voice was husky, it was because her heart was literally beating in the middle of her throat.

"I'm glad you called," he said. "I wanted to know if you had called the telephone company to get a new number."

"First thing this morning," she replied, smiling. "And this time I asked for an unlisted number."

"Good girl," he approved with a soft laugh. He was silent a moment and then said, "I'd like to stop by and see you on my way home."

She smiled. "How about for dinner, unless you have other plans?"

"Dinner it is."

They talked a few more minutes and then said good-bye. Lauren resettled Freddy and leaned back in her chair, greedily hoarding every precious word Colby had said to her.

At last she went into the kitchen to tell her grandmother that they would be having another guest for dinner.

"Who?" Jill inquired with polite interest. She was sitting at the table, her homework spread out in front of her, and by the looks of it she had accomplished a great deal in a very short span of time.

"Lieutenant Colby Sherman." Lauren didn't miss the look of surprised dismay that flitted across Donnie's lean features.

"A cop." He scowled.

107

"A badge-carrying, gun-toting, bona-fide lieutenant," Lauren declared, nodding, all the while wondering why this should bother the youngster. He had paled considerably; the freckles that normally darkened only when he'd been too long in the sun were standing out like moles.

There was a strange look in Jill's brown eyes, and the smile that faintly curled one corner of her mouth seemed smug. "He's coming here for dinner?"

"He's a good friend of Laurie's," Catherine piped up before Lauren could reply, cautioning, "and I want you both to be on your best behavior at dinner."

"I hate cops," Donnie snarled.

"Shut up, Donnie," Jill said. "He's a friend of Dad's, remember?"

This was news to Lauren. "Oh, really?"

Jill looked up at Lauren and smiled brightly. "They've been friends ever since the lieutenant started dating Anne Mulrooney, the secretary over at the Chamber of Commerce. That's where Dad met him."

A shaft of jealousy darted through her, and it was only then that Lauren finally admitted to herself that she was in love with Colby Sherman. Jealously, possessively, fiercely, in love with the man.

She returned to the living room in a pensive mood.

Sensing her mood, Maggie worked quietly and efficiently through what remained of her shift while Lauren spent her time working on her ledgers.

When Lauren heard a car stopping in front of her house at a quarter past six, she rushed to the door, hoping it would be Colby. But when she opened the door, she found Jeanne and Rob standing on the porch.

"Oh, it's only you," she said by way of greeting, and laughed softly.

"Oh, you were expecting Robert Redford?" Jeanne shot

back, her green eyes, so much like Lauren's, glinting with amusement.

"Will I do?" Smiling indulgently, Rob leaned down and kissed Lauren on the cheek.

"Will *I* do?" a very familiar voice echoed Rob's words from somewhere behind him. As though they had rehearsed this little scenario, Rob and Jeanne stepped aside and allowed Colby to precede them into the house.

A charcoal-gray silk shirt stretched across his broad chest and hugged his slender torso as it tapered down into the narrow waist of his black slacks. He approached Lauren slowly, creating tension between them simply by moving in that lithe, controlled way of his.

"I'm happy you could join us," she murmured.

He took her hand. "I'm glad you invited me."

His touch singed her flesh, and as he leaned forward to touch his lips to her cheek, Lauren inhaled sharply, drawing in his now-familiar spicy aftershave.

"I wasn't aware you knew each other," she said, looking at Rob, then at Jeanne, noting that they were both looking a trifle smug.

"Colby and I go back a long way," Rob offered, his heavy-lidded turquoise eyes gleaming with amusement. Tossing a look over at Jeanne that spoke volumes, he added, "We ran into each other quite often at Chamber meetings."

"So I'm told," Lauren murmured. Looking up at Jeanne she said, "The kids are in the kitchen, stuffing their faces with Grandma's cookies and milk. I don't think they'll be wanting dinner, but you're welcome to stay if you haven't planned anything."

"I was hoping you'd ask," Jeanne said, laughing as she headed toward the kitchen, leaving behind a subtle hint of a very expensive perfume.

"I think I'll go get some of those cookies before they're all gone," Rob said, discreetly leaving Lauren and Colby alone in the living room.

"And now that we're finally alone . . ." Smiling wickedly, Colby placed his hands on Lauren's shoulders and very gently drew her to him. He didn't take her into his arms, and he didn't kiss her.

Lauren glanced up, confused, expectant.

"Have there been any calls today?" he whispered, his expression almost frighteningly sober.

Lauren shook her head.

"That's good." He stood for a moment just looking at her, a contemplative expression in his eyes. And then he smiled. "I don't think you'll be having any more trouble."

"Oh, I hope you're right. I don't think I could take much more of his foul talk."

He drew her to him then, and kissed her. "I wouldn't want you to take any more of his smutty talk," he whispered against her hair. Lauren snuggled into his embrace, feeling warm and secure with his arms surrounding her.

"I hear you have a full house again. Are you sure you want me to stay for dinner?" Two fingers lightly touching her chin, he urged her face up. "Or, would they mind if you and I took off by ourselves?" He smiled persuasively. "As much as I enjoy the councilman, your sister and grandmother, I would much prefer having you all to myself."

His wishes echoed her feelings, but Lauren found herself shaking her head. She couldn't leave, particularly not after her grandmother had gone to so much trouble to prepare a delicious dinner for them.

"I'm sorry. I wish I could, but I can't. Grandma would never forgive me."

He nodded. "You can't blame a guy for trying," he said, a faint smile on his mouth. It was the expression in his eyes—slightly cynical and hard—that made Lauren feel uneasy.

"I'm sorry," she repeated, and then turned from him, pretending interest in something outside the window.

Colby took a swift, silent breath and, folding his arms

negligently over his chest, studied Lauren's profile, aware, back in his mind somewhere, that she was unhappy.

"Something bothering you?" he finally asked, only idly curious.

"No," she lied. "I was just listening to the chatter coming from the kitchen and wondering if we ought to join them."

He flashed a glance in the direction of the kitchen and shook his head. "They don't sound like they miss us. How about offering me a drink instead?"

Lauren nodded. "What would you prefer? I have wine and beer."

"He'd probably prefer Scotch on the rocks, but he's getting beer," Jeanne announced with a laugh as she came forward with a beer bottle in one hand and a wineglass in the other. "I know what you like," she said, holding out the wine to Lauren.

Somehow, Lauren didn't think Jeanne was referring to the wine. She smiled.

"You've been keeping secrets from me, Laurie," Jeanne teased in a hushed whisper as she took Lauren's glass from her and sipped at the wine. Curiosity gleamed in her eyes, but there was something else too. It was almost as though she were accusing Lauren of purposely keeping her acquaintance with Colby hidden because of some deep, dark secret.

"I'm entitled, Big Sister," Lauren retorted with a short laugh.

"Gramma says dinner's ready," Jill announced just as Jeanne was about to say something else. Lauren would be eternally grateful for the interruption.

"Then let's go in before she decides we're not interested." Smiling at Jill, Jeanne slipped an arm around the girl's slender shoulders and held out a hand to Donnie.

Lauren noticed that Jill's shoulders went rigid under the burden of Jeanne's arm. And Donnie ignored the outstretched hand.

Damn kids! she thought furiously, wishing she could

crack their heads together for being so spiteful toward Jeanne.

Rob watched until Jeanne and the kids had disappeared into the kitchen, and then he turned to face Lauren. Noting the frowning expression that marred her lovely features, he smiled with understanding. "Don't worry about Jeanne. She'll turn them around. All they need is a little time."

"Or a good swift kick in the pants?" Lauren suggested dryly.

Colby laughed. Startled, Lauren turned to stare at him. "Bloodthirsty little thing, aren't you?" he teased. Smiling down at her, he asked Rob, "Did you know she had such a violent streak running through her?"

"I wouldn't worry," Rob returned, laughing. "Her bark is really worse than her bite."

"I heard somewhere that it's her claws I have to worry about."

"Claws, teeth, feet. I have it on good authority that she's a very dirty fighter."

Colby grinned, thoroughly enjoying himself. "I think I can handle her."

Lauren glanced from one to the other as the men bantered about her, feeling as though she were watching a Ping-Pong game. She wasn't too thrilled with the way they were discussing her, but she had better sense than to try defending herself.

Two things she had learned growing up with two older sisters. Taking up the gauntlet was futile when she was caught between two adversaries, and indifference was a perfectly satisfactory defense.

"I think I'll go in to dinner before I incur Grandma's wrath," she said softly, smiling sweetly up at the two men. "Would you like to join me?"

"I have a feeling if we don't, she'll go in without us," Colby said to Rob, and then in unison they each took an arm and hustled her into the kitchen.

112

Dinner was a lively affair. Normally, Lauren didn't enjoy political or religious discussions, but tonight she was perfectly content to sit and listen to Colby and Rob hashing over the pros and cons of banning cruising in the city's streets.

"It's not fair!" Jill interjected at one point, glaring at her father with the same ferocity that she directed at Colby. "You used to have the same kind of fun when you were in your teens, so why is it so wrong for us to enjoy the same things?"

Lauren waited, remembering how often she had uttered similar questions only to have them answered with "And who said that life was fair?"

Resting his elbows on the table, Rob very carefully steepled his fingers and, looking over them at Jill, explained, "When we were teens, Jill, we didn't have as many cars on the road."

"We had a different attitude too," Colby interjected without rancor, "toward our authority figures, whether they were our parents, the school administration, or . . . the police." He fixed Donnie with a long, searching look. "What we had were advantages, Jill, not privileges," he continued gently, smiling into the girl's mulish expression. "I'm not saying that you don't have a legitimate gripe, but it's your own generation that's responsible for losing you those advantages."

"We haven't done anything to deserve this," Jill defended furiously. "My friends and I are very careful when we're in cars. We don't drink, we don't do drugs, we don't speed, we aren't destructive. So why should we be punished along with everyone else who might do all or some of those things?" Her eyes were literally snapping with fury.

"Unfortunately, darling, the innocent ones like you are swept right along with the crowd," Jeanne explained, reaching out to pat Jill's clenched fist. "I know it's not fair, but that's the way life is."

Ouch! Lauren thought, cringing inwardly. If Jill hated hearing those words as much as she herself had when she was that age, she had every right to start throwing things. But to Lauren's, as well as everyone else's, surprise, the girl merely smiled thinly and promptly removed her hand from under Jeanne's.

"I remember when Laurie was your age," Rob said, smiling wickedly at Lauren. "She drove Matthew and Lina crazy every weekend. She insisted on having the same curfew as her sisters."

"And she wanted to date at fourteen because she had several of the senior boys after her," Jeanne added with a short, happy laugh. "I remember that Mom wanted to send her to Aunt Marty in Boston after she caught her sneaking out the window one night after curfew."

"Would you both stop using me as a bad example?" Lauren demanded.

"But you're not a bad example," Jeanne denied hotly. "Think about it. You've got everything you want, a house, a business, a healthy bank account—"

"All because she finally learned to work *within* the system," Rob interjected smoothly.

All through this Colby had remained silent. Under the guise of idle curiosity he studied the children while the adults were busy enumerating Lauren's assets and successes. And he noted the animosity in Donnie's eyes each time the boy looked at Lauren.

He leaned back in his chair, quietly observant, allowing the conversation to swirl around him while his professional eye took in and catalogued the emotions that were conveyed so clearly on Donnie's face. Ironically, he had come to understand why Donnie—and Jill too—had grown to resent Lauren. It was obvious that their father had a special fondness for her, a feeling the two teens obviously didn't think he had for them.

And the way they carry on about you, he thought, looking

114

fondly at Lauren. *It's a wonder there's not a halo brightly gleaming over your head.*

"Did you say something?" Lauren asked quietly, looking into his eyes, wondering at the strange expression she found there.

"Only that I'm going to have to get going."

Lauren glanced around the table, wishing that she'd had a little more time alone with Colby. "Excuse me, please. Colby has to go, and I'm going to see him to the door."

Chairs scraped against the floor as they both stood. After Colby had thanked Catherine for a delicious dinner and said good-night to the rest, they went out onto the porch to say good-night in private.

CHAPTER EIGHT

"Alone at last," Colby murmured, sliding his arms around Lauren's waist the instant the door had closed behind them and they were alone on the darkened porch. Slowly, he gathered her to him, holding her lightly, for the moment content just to hold her.

Lauren tipped her head back to look into his eyes. She found only herself reflected in them, her own needs mirrored in their darkened depths. She waited, breath held, hoping he would trust her enough to tell her what he was feeling.

"I can't tell you how wonderful this evening with you has been." His mouth brushed across her forehead, over long-lashed lids that trembled closed, and soft pink lips that parted in anticipation. "I could learn to love being part of your nutty family," he added, brushing tiny kisses all over her face.

It was not exactly what she had been hoping to hear, but it would do for the time being. Lauren leaned into him, rested her cheek against his chest, and listened, entranced, to the rapid beating of his heart.

For long, long moments they held each other without speaking, their bodies silhouetted as one against the purple-blackness of night. And then he tilted her face to his, her name a song against her lips until she opened her mouth to his, like a flower greedily drinking in a soft summer rain.

The kiss left them both shaking.

In the comparative quiet of the night Colby's sigh

sounded ragged. "Do you know what you're doing to me?" His voice was a barely discernible whisper breathed across her mouth. His fingers worked their way around her throat, winding gently into the tumble of blond waves that fell across her shoulders. "If I don't take myself home right now, I won't be held responsible for what might happen to you," he said in a much stronger tone.

Caught off guard, Lauren made a small, inarticulate sound in her throat and laughed shakily as she stepped back. "I can just see the headlines now," she teased, her voice embarrassingly husky. She made double quotation marks in the air and quipped, "Head of local gendarmes goes berserk on mystery woman's porch."

He smiled, thankful that she was helping to put them both back on comfortable ground. "Taking into account that no two papers report any incident in exactly the same way, we could count on several conflicting reports. Some would probably read, 'Citizen Complaining of Harassment Calls Gets Mauled by Investigating Officer.' And those would probably be closer to the truth." He laughed softly, deeply, before pulling her to him again for a final kiss.

"I'll call you tomorrow," he called over his shoulder as he went to his car.

Lauren waited until his car had turned onto the cross street, and then she went back into the house.

Later that night, after the dinner dishes were done and Catherine was satisfied with the way the kitchen looked, they retired to the living room with a cup of tea each.

"Colby is such a nice man," Catherine said, sinking to the couch, curling her legs under herself as she rested back against the cushions. "I really like him."

"So do I."

Taking a sip of her tea, Catherine glanced over the rim of the cup at Lauren and smiled. "Don't let him get away from you, honey. He's a good man."

"Yes, he is." Lauren set her cup down on the floor and

removed her sandals. She stretched her legs out, flexed her toes, and grinned. Grandma was trying to matchmake and wasn't even trying to hide it. "And, given time, he just might end up being more, but for now, I am perfectly content having him just as a friend."

Disappointment made Catherine's voice sound oddly strained. "One bad apple doesn't necessarily ruin the entire crop, Laurie. Don't let your experience with the Tolan boy cloud your judgment. After all, it's been several years—"

"I left Johnny Tolan back in college, Gram," Lauren interjected swiftly, a small wrinkle forming between her eyes. "Along with his anarchistic leanings and his contempt for the working classes." She hadn't thought of Johnny in a long time, and she was sorry he had been brought into the conversation now. She'd loved him deeply, fiercely, and leaving him had hurt like hell. But he wasn't the reason she had dated infrequently since opening her business.

"If I have to have a reason for not going all-out to hook Colby Sherman, it will have to be that I am satisfied with my life the way it is right now." She forced a smile that faded quickly with her grandmother's response.

"Don't wait too long to make up your mind. I have a feeling that Colby has already made his up, and he strikes me as a man who stops at nothing to get what he wants."

Things were getting a little too heavy. "Oh, boy, am I exhausted," Lauren said, faking a yawn as she slowly rose to her feet. "All things considered, it's been quite a day, hasn't it?" As she started out of the room to go put her cup and saucer in the sink, she heard her grandmother muttering something she couldn't distinguish.

"I agree wholeheartedly," Lauren said, giggling. "Now, what did you say?"

"That you have a nasty habit of changing the subject whenever it suits you and running away when you're losing."

"Like I said, I agree wholeheartedly." Lauren gave her

grandmother a gamine grin and was rewarded with a re-proachful look. She sighed. "I'm sorry, Gram. I know I'm being contrary, but it's only because I don't know myself yet what is there and what isn't in my relationship with Colby, or even what I really want from it." She walked back to the couch and leaned over to kiss Catherine on the cheek. "And now, I'm going to bed. Good night."

Catherine reached up a hand and gently patted Lauren's cheek. All was forgiven. "You go on, dear. I'm going to stay up and read for a little while."

"Don't stay up too late," Lauren cautioned, and then she took the cup into the kitchen, ran water over it, and went to bed.

Tuesday passed without incident. Lauren collapsed into bed at ten o'clock that night with a sigh of relief. There had been no harassing calls. And her grandmother's scheme seemed to be working. Jill and Donnie were not falling over themselves being loving toward her, but she had confused them with her gentle treatment. And if that was what it took to make her life more bearable, she was willing to go all out to keep them off their feet. Of course, taking them out for an afternoon snack every day was probably going to break her.

Lauren was getting ready for bed when the insistent clamor of the telephone arrested her movements. Her fingers stilled, and for a horrifying moment, the old fear returned. She considered letting the phone ring, but then she remembered that her grandmother was visiting and would probably go answer it.

"This had better be good!" she muttered, bolstering her courage with a small dose of righteous anger.

It was.

Colby's voice flowed warmly into her ear. "Did I interrupt something? You sound a little agitated."

"Only because I thought you were the obscene caller," Lauren returned with a laugh.

"He hasn't been calling again?" His voice was sharp with concern.

"No, thank goodness."

His laugh was soft, relaxed, thankful. "I'm glad.

"Now, what I called about was lunch, tomorrow, about twelve?"

"I'd love to."

"Great. I'll pick you up at quarter of." He said good-bye and hung up.

The corners of her mouth dimpled as Lauren lowered the receiver. It was going to be a wonderful Wednesday!

As it turned out, it wasn't. She was up to her elbows in cookie dough when the doorbell rang. Lauren reached for a towel to wipe her arms, but before she had a chance to leave the kitchen, Colby strode into the room with a bouquet of red roses.

"Your grandmother let me in," he said. "It's nice that she can handle the switchboard to give you a break."

"Lovely," Lauren said, both to the roses and to the fact that her grandmother was so helpful, then went warm all over as his hands settled around her waist and he brought her to him for a kiss. She tingled to the tips of her toes, but before she could get too comfortable in his arms, he set her away from him.

"Thank you for the roses. They're lovely."

He smiled. "My pleasure." He looked at her, really looked, and then he started laughing. "If you could only see how you look!"

She had a vague idea that she was wearing more dough on herself than she had put into the cookies. "It's not my fault that you came sooner than I expected you," she grumbled, but she smiled. She didn't care that he was early, only that he was there with her.

"No. No, it's not. But don't let it bother you. You look adorable to me." He laughed softly as he bent to kiss her again, and then he stepped back and turned to go.

120

"If you'll give me half an hour—"

"I can't, Lauren, I'm sorry." He frowned. "I know I promised to take you to lunch, but I'm on my way right now to make an arrest."

Fear clutched at her stomach, her throat. "Be careful, please," she choked out, but he didn't hear her because he was hurrying away. A second or so later she heard him saying good-bye to her grandmother, and then the sound of the front door closing behind him signaled his departure.

A vague uneasiness shadowed her activities the rest of the day, a real fear that he might be in danger, that she might never see him again.

When she picked up the children at their respective schools late that afternoon, she insisted on taking them across town for their snack. To her surprise neither child objected.

Fifteen minutes later she drove into the parking lot, feeling more relaxed than she'd felt all afternoon. The police station was on the way to the restaurant, and she had spied Colby's car parked on the lot. Since he had been driving it when he went to her house, she assumed that his arrest had been successful. Hopefully, it had also been uneventful.

Five minutes after they were seated at their table, Jill remarked, "Was he the reason you wanted to come out here?" nodding her head to direct Lauren's attention to the tall, good-looking male walking toward them.

Turning, Lauren caught sight of the man who had been dominating all her thoughts lately. Looking for all the world as though he owned the place, Colby was smiling as he approached their table.

"I noticed your car parked outside, so I decided to stop and treat you all to a milk shake." He lowered his body onto the padded bench beside Lauren, ignoring the murderous look Donnie flashed at him.

"If you don't mind, I'd rather just have a glass of iced tea," Jill said softly, smiling up at Colby in apology.

He nodded. "What about you, Donnie? A milk shake? A banana split?"

"I'd better just have iced tea too. Mom'll kill me if I ruin my appetite for dinner."

I doubt it, thought Colby, but he nodded in agreement. And when the waitress came to take their order, he asked for four iced teas.

"How's it going?" he whispered to Lauren.

"Nice, now that you're here."

Colby's gaze moved over her face slowly, drinking in every lovely detail, and when he finally spoke, there was a strange quality in his voice. "I'm glad to be here, with you." Perhaps later, certainly before she had a chance to read about it in the newspapers, or see it on the eleven o'clock news, he would tell her about the harrowing experience he'd had that morning.

It was a delightful afternoon. Happy to be in possession of life and limb, Colby went out of his way to be amusing, to put Lauren, as well as the children, at ease. By the time he walked them out to Lauren's car, he knew he could count Jill among his fans. The jury was still out on Donnie, however. The boy had a harder shell to crack than the best of Maine lobsters.

"Call you later," Colby murmured, stifling a desire to take Lauren into his arms as he opened her car door. He wasn't holding back because the children were present. He was just afraid that if he held her, his embrace would be too fierce, and Lauren would surely suspect there was something bothering him.

"I'll be home." Lauren slid in under the wheel, waited until he was walking to his own car before leaving the lot. She was moodily silent all the way home, plagued with a strange doubt she couldn't define.

"Do you think you'll be needing more help later on?" Jill asked shyly as they were walking into the house.

"In what, hon?" The endearment was automatic.

122

"With your phone service."

Lauren groaned inwardly as she glanced across the room at the switchboard. She was painfully conscious of the expectant expression on Jill's face, and realized that she had to be extremely careful in discouraging the girl from any idea of working for her. She didn't want to destroy what little good she had accomplished in the last couple of days.

"Not for a long while, Jill. Why? Are you looking for a job?"

Jill's slender shoulders went up in a shrug. "I just wondered."

"Well, if you're ever in the market for a part-time job, maybe I can guide you to someone who's hiring."

"Lauren?" Jill grasped Lauren's arm before she could escape into the kitchen. "Would you?"

"Of course."

"And would you also talk to your sis—to Mom? She'll listen to you. Make her see that there's nothing wrong with me wanting to do something more than just go to school and come home to help Donnie with his homework."

Lauren was properly stunned. But she managed to keep it from showing in her voice. "All right. I'll see what I can do. But I'm not promising anything." She smiled gently and then slowly moved away. *Will wonders never cease?* she thought as she went into her bedroom.

In the next couple of days Lauren noticed that both children spent a lot of time talking to Maggie about the answering service. Jill was very curious about the entire operation, while Donnie seemed almost obsessed with learning the names of the businesses that used the service.

Sunlight woke Lauren, pale-gold streamers that stole into her room and bathed her face with their gentle warmth. She murmured drowsily and reached out for the extra pillow to lay across her face and block the light. She wasn't ready to get up.

And then she remembered it was Friday. D-Day. The last day she would have to go pick up the kids after school. The last day of her grandmother's visit. And that night Colby had invited her to dinner in San Francisco. After dinner they were going dancing.

She sat up quickly, smiling, and reached to the foot of her bed for her robe. Slipping it on as she left the bed, she went into the kitchen to start the coffee.

Catherine was at the stove, fixing breakfast. And the air in the kitchen was filled with the aroma of frying bacon and grilled onions.

Lauren's stomach churned with the thought of forcing herself to eat breakfast just to please her grandmother. Her "Good morning, Gram," was discernibly grumpy, but Catherine seemed not to notice.

Forty-five minutes later Lauren was in the middle of passing on appointments she had made for a free-lance photographer when her doorbell rang. Slanting a quick look toward the door, she wondered who her caller could be and whether he would still be there when she finished what she was doing.

"I'll get it, dear," Catherine said as she hurried past her.

When she came back, she had a florist's box in her hands. "It's for you, honey," she said, handing the box to an astonished Lauren.

The gift had to come from Colby. Lauren went warm all over with delight. Her hands trembled as she eagerly tore off the ribbon and pulled off the lid to expose a dozen lovely long-stemmed red roses lying in a bed of dark-green tissue.

The card read: *To keep you company until I can be with you.* There was no signature on the card, but Lauren knew the roses were from Colby.

When at last she became aware that Catherine was looking at her, Lauren glanced up.

"From Colby." She laughed softly.

"That's what I thought," came the amused reply. "Would you like me to put them in water for you?"

Lauren looked down at the roses again, and if not for the thorns, she would surely have pressed them to her breast. "Yes, please." She relinquished the box into her grandmother's hands and reluctantly returned her attention to the switchboard.

The day seemed to drag on forever. Lauren knew it was because she was eager for evening and Colby to arrive. She tried to relax, to concentrate only on what she was doing, to the exclusion of all else. But it was futile. Her thoughts kept going back to Colby and the roses.

She greeted day's end and her brother-in-law and sister with great relief.

"We know you have a date, so we won't hold you up," Jeanne said as she sailed past her and went in search of the kids and Catherine.

Rob lingered by the door. "We can't tell you how grateful we are that you were here to help us out when we needed you." He kissed her on the cheek. "Thanks, Laurie. For taking care of them certainly, but most of all for the after-school treats. That fell in the category of 'above and beyond.'"

Lauren was pleased. "I'll have to admit that it was fun for me too." She smiled up at him. "They gave me a perfect excuse to go on an ice-cream binge without feeling guilty about it."

Just then, Jeanne reappeared, with the kids and Catherine trailing behind her. "I guess we're ready," she said to Rob. Jill was carrying Catherine's suitcases, and Donnie was loaded down with their schoolbooks and other paraphernalia.

Fifteen minutes later Lauren was in the shower, singing as she washed her hair, happily looking forward to being with Colby.

When Colby arrived precisely at eight o'clock, Lauren

125

was grateful she had taken more care than usual with her appearance. Elegantly attired in gray slacks, navy blazer, and a shirt and tie, the man was breathtaking. Lauren's heartbeat quickened. The slow, slumberous gaze he ran over her didn't help her breathing any, and she had difficulty even in saying hello.

"Hello yourself," he murmured, and, closing the inches that separated them, he caught her by the waist and lifted her up to his mouth. A shaft of sensation shot through her, and she felt a thrill clear down to the tips of her toes. His mouth was warm, moist, insistent, and, with a sigh, Lauren opened her mouth to his exploration.

Slowly, reluctantly, Colby's mouth released her. Then, with his hands still around her waist, he drew back. "If we want to get to the city at all tonight, I think maybe we'd better get going."

Lauren nodded. "I'll just get my wrap."

Colby watched her moving toward the sofa and again felt the sting of desire. The gown she wore looked fabulous as it molded over her curves and contours, the bright turquoise enhancing the green of her eyes. Yet all he could think of was taking it off her and sating his hunger in the warm softness of her body.

A shudder tore through his body at the slow, sensual gait that she used in getting to him, and for a second he closed his eyes, willing his desire to go away. He felt her hand touching his arm, and with a sigh that never left his mouth, he opened his eyes and looked down at her, perfectly composed now.

"Did I forget to tell you how beautiful you look?"

"Do you like this?" She sketched a small pirouette, the wide skirt of her gown swirling, giving him a tantalizing view of her upper legs.

"I like." His lips curved in a tiny, teasing smile. "The contents of the package as well as the wrapping."

Lauren swallowed, feeling as if she were totally out of her

depth. As she started to drape her silvery-gray shawl around her shoulders, she felt his hands taking it from her.

"Allow me," he murmured, and she turned obediently to allow him to cover her bare shoulders with the velvet triangle.

Colby drew in a deep, restorative breath. Then, giving in to an urge he didn't want to control, he caught her chin with his fingers, tilted her face up, and brushed her mouth against his in a soft, tantalizing kiss. He released her quickly, giving himself no time to yield to a much stronger desire.

A small moan slipped through her trembling lips. Lauren felt her knees quivering and gladly took the arm he offered for support.

In the car Lauren was quiet, thoughtful, and Colby was grateful for the silence. He had a lot on his mind. He wanted her, wanted her more than he had ever wanted anyone else. But, he finally admitted, he was afraid of making a commitment.

Lauren heard him sigh and slanted a look at him, quickly registering the grim smile that cut across his generous mouth. Whatever his thoughts were, they were not pleasant, she decided, and certainly none of her business, so she wouldn't pry. She turned her head and stared out the window.

"Did you hear that someone wanted to paint Coit Tower to, uh, beautify it?" he asked, finally breaking the heavy silence that had hung over them all the way into the city.

"All in the name of progress," Lauren added with a brief laugh, a sound without mirth or warmth. "I'll have to admit that I wouldn't want to see it changed."

"Nor would I."

Giving his precious car into the care of an eager attendant, Colby led her out of the garage, his hand just lightly pressing the small of her waist.

It was a beautiful night, clear, if a bit cool. Lauren drew

127

the ends of her shawl together and carefully knotted them over her breasts to keep it from slipping off her shoulders.

Colby was very conscious of the heads that turned their way as they were being led to their table—mostly male, the expression on their faces easy to understand. They more than approved of the lady with him. They envied him.

He smiled in amusement as he casually slipped a proprietary arm around her slender waist prior to helping her to her chair. As he went to his own chair, he flashed a glance around the room and noticed that there were still a few faces turned toward them. A large, magnanimous smile softened his features. He could afford to be magnanimous. Lauren Shayler belonged to him, and after tonight, even she would know it.

CHAPTER NINE

The night was like a lovely dream, a beautiful fantasy that Lauren never wanted to see coming to an end.

And it was all due to the man whose arms held her closely as they danced. Lauren tilted her head up and back, smiling.

"You dance marvelously well for a police lieutenant," she teased. "And here I've been thinking that all lieutenants had flat feet and walked with a heavy step." Her hair seemed to gather and trap the light as she tossed her head back with a laugh. Her eyes, fixed on his mobile mouth, glittered like precious gems with the light dancing over her face.

"I could always step on your toes now and then just to prove your theory," he offered generously.

She gave him a breathtaking smile. "Not necessary," she said quickly. "I happen to like the way you dance."

"It's all due to the lovely creature in my arms," he said in a soft, velvety voice that sent a shiver of sensation spiraling through her entire body. "She makes me feel like I'm dancing on a cloud."

She, too, felt as if she were floating on a cloud. Smiling her thanks for the compliment, Lauren leaned her forehead against his chest and drew a deep breath, happy with him, with herself, with life in general. She relished the silken softness of his white shirt and the warmth that seeped through it to touch her brow.

The music slowly faded away, but for a moment the crush of human bodies on the dance floor prevented Lauren and

Colby from returning to their table. Bending his head, he brushed his mouth across hers and whispered, "We can leave whenever you wish."

A shiver slithered down the length of her spine at the emotion that hoarsened his voice. Lauren knew he was eager to take her home, and the reason why. As his desires marched right alongside hers, she decided she wanted to leave right then.

At last they were able to leave the floor. Going directly to their table, Lauren gathered her shawl and the turquoise pumps she had discarded after their first dance.

As he dropped a couple of bills onto the table, Colby noticed that Lauren was carefully looking around, as if to memorize the beauty that surrounded them. "We'll have to come back," he said.

She smiled. "The dance floor might not be the largest I've seen, but the rest is marvelous," she murmured, draping her shawl carelessly over her shoulders. Balancing herself on one foot and then the other, she slipped her shoes back on.

Through the huge faceted windows she could see a large slice of the city, the lights blinking and winking like so many Christmas lights. Surrounded by windows, the Oz Room of the Westin St. Francis Hotel offered its guests a lovely, panoramic view of San Francisco. Lauren slowly approached a window for one last look.

"Beautiful, isn't it?" she asked, looking over her shoulder at Colby as he joined her.

"Breathtaking," he murmured, but he wasn't looking down at the scene that lay at their feet.

Lauren's mouth went dry, and her heart quickened its beat, began hammering almost painfully against her ribs. Under his prolonged, appreciative study of her features, she felt herself blushing. Something tightened in the region of her lower abdomen. And as his fingers curled around her arm and they started walking toward the elevator, she found

130

herself wishing she could be bold enough to suggest they take a room for what remained of the night.

She was vaguely aware of a crispness in the air that fanned their faces as they walked back to the garage, but with Colby's muscular arm lying across her shoulders and his warm body touching hers as they walked, it could have been freezing and Lauren wouldn't have minded.

The silence that fell over them almost as soon as they were settled in the car was charged with tension. Lauren clasped her hands together on her lap to still their nervousness. She felt breathless with excitement; her every nerve end tingled with anticipation.

Get hold of yourself! she instructed her jittery self sternly, and turned her attention to the dark landscape flashing past the window of the speeding car.

The ride back to her house seemed shorter, but Lauren suspected it was because Colby was in more of a rush to get there than he'd been to get to the restaurant.

He drove the car up into her driveway and, turning off the ignition with a sharp twist of his hand, shifted to face Lauren. Resting one elbow on the steering wheel, he searched her quiet features a long time before he spoke.

"You've been extremely quiet all the way home. Is something wrong?"

How could she tell him that the reason she had been so quiet was that her heart had seemed to be lodged in her throat, making it difficult to breathe, let alone talk? And her wits were so scattered even now that she was afraid to talk for fear of sounding like a total imbecile.

So she gave a small shake of her head. "I like to be quiet once in a while," she murmured, feeling breathless as his eyes focused on her mouth.

"I thought maybe you were tired. I have a feeling that like me, this is the first time you've been out dancing in a long time."

"No. I'm not tired. Well, only my feet," she amended, and they both laughed.

Their laughter cleared the air, and with a smile Colby left the car to go around and help her out. When their hands touched, he felt a thrill shooting up his arm, and he held his breath.

Lauren had her own problems. Her knees seemed to have no control at all, and as she left the car, she fell against him.

"If you'll give me your key, I'll get the door."

While Lauren was digging into her small beaded bag for her house key, she heard the phone ringing. She purposely delayed finding the key, hoping that the stupid thing would stop ringing before they got into the house.

But its ring was insistent, and though she tried to ignore it, she couldn't.

"If you'll excuse me," she murmured, stepping away from Colby, switching the light on as she moved through the foyer.

The hesitant voice that answered her greeting was as polite as it was unfamiliar. "I'm sorry to disturb you, miss, but I'd like to speak to the lieutenant. He left this number—"

Disappointment, frustration, anger, melded together, and for a second Lauren was tempted to slam the receiver down. But she mentally counted to ten, took a deep breath, and turned to face Colby.

"I think it's one of your men."

Colby's strong features contorted into a mask of disappointment. "Lord, I was hoping they wouldn't need me tonight." With an apologetic smile he added, "I'm sorry. I left your number in case they needed me. And I guess they do."

But I'll bet not half as much as I do, Lauren complained silently, and turned her back to him, not so much because she wanted to let him speak to his man in private but because she didn't want him to see how disappointed she was. Why hadn't he left the restaurant number, or the lounge's?

132

Why did it have to be hers? And why the devil did he have to be on call?

Her legs were stiff, her back was rigid with anger, as she took her disappointment into the kitchen for a drink of water.

She didn't bother turning on a light, but crept cautiously across the room to the cupboard for a glass. She filled it with water and took it to the table. It was there that Colby found her a few minutes later.

"Do you mind if I turn on a light?" he questioned from the doorway. He blinked his eyes to quicken their adjustment to the dark, and then pierced the darkness to find her. He saw her sitting with her back to him and didn't miss the small shrug that lifted one of her slim shoulders.

"Please do." Lauren forced a smile, glad that her voice had sounded normal. She knew she had no legitimate reason to be angry with him. After all, she had no claims on him. Still, she had to curl her hands into fists on her lap to maintain a forced-calm demeanor.

"I'm sorry, Lauren." His fingers found the light switch, flipped it on. As the room was flooded with light, Colby strode across it, pulled out a chair, and sat down facing her.

"I hope you can believe that I had planned a much nicer end to our evening." One long hand covered her fists, curled around them.

"I believe you," she murmured, keeping her face downbent, her eyes idly studying the hand that covered hers.

"When I invited you to dinner tonight, I had completely forgotten that I was on call. We've had a bit of a problem at the station, with vacations coming due at the same time that other officers are out with some kind of flu."

He released her hands and caught her chin in his fingers, tilting her face to his. Lauren held her breath, keeping her eyes fixed on his, watching as his head bent toward her. She felt a tingling in her fingers, a soothing warmth flowing through her body, easing away the remnants of her anger.

Feeling somehow that if she didn't stop the kiss, she would make a fool of herself and ask him to stay with her a little bit longer, she pulled her lips away from his with a heavy sigh.

"You don't want to keep 'em waiting." She didn't know exactly what he was going back to the station to do, but at the moment she was too preoccupied with her own feelings to ask what it was that was taking him away from her.

"No. No, I don't. But I don't have to leave this very minute." His fingers caressed her cheek, brushed lightly across her mouth, took a wispy tendril of blond hair that lay across her cheek and gently wound it around his fingers. He used it to urge her face toward his again. His mouth descended upon hers again, hard, insistent, demanding, as it moved across her lips.

No, she thought. She had to put a stop to his before he took her only far enough to leave her wanting more. Trembling, breathless, hating what she was doing, she slipped her hands between them to push him away. "Please don't, Colby."

Slowly, he went back in the chair, breathing hard, his hands trembling as he drew them away from her and clasped them together over one knee. Smoldering, passion-darkened eyes roamed her features; searching for what, Lauren couldn't tell.

"I'm very tired," she said, rising swiftly to her feet, wanting only to see the back of him going through the front door. "And you shouldn't keep your people waiting."

"You're right." He sounded defeated. "I shouldn't keep the public waiting." And as he stood, he added, "To hell with my private life, as long as I do what the people expect of me, right?"

Lauren turned sharply around to stare at him.

"I'm sorry," he said roughly. "I guess I'm more tired than I realized."

He couldn't be any more sorry than she, Lauren thought, feeling vaguely tearful as she led the way to the front door.

Consumed with a need to let out her frustrations in a good old-fashioned crying jag, she showed more haste than tact as she threw open the door and mumbled, "Good night, Lieutenant."

In speechless confusion Colby stood on the threshold, looking down at her unhappy expression. He ached to take her in his arms, to hold her until that desolate look vanished from her eyes, but he knew he dared not touch her. If he did, he would not want to leave her. And he had to go. Duty called, he thought, his mouth moving in a cynical downward curve.

"I'll call you soon, all right?"

Lauren nodded, afraid to trust her voice. There was a burning sensation just behind her eyes, and a dryness in her throat, warning signs that very soon she would probably burst into tears of self-pity.

Sunday was as depressing as Saturday had been. Not only was she still suffering from her disappointment of Friday night, but she also received the first obscene phone call of the week.

This is all I need to make my day complete, she thought wearily, cutting the creep off in midsentence. She glared at the switchboard, as though it were responsible for her bad humor.

Not one to dwell on her misfortunes, Lauren decided she needed people around her to keep her from giving in to the doldrums. She went to her personal phone and quickly dialed Jeanne's number.

"Hi, Jeanne, this is Lauren."

"Hi, sweetie, what's up?"

"Me, and I'm lonesome."

"I see. Colby must be on duty."

Lauren groaned softly, but Jeanne took it as answer in the affirmative and, in a comforting tone, invited her to brunch.

Firmly resolving to keep Friday evening private between

herself and Colby, Lauren swiftly dressed and was in her car and on her way to the Hunter residence twenty minutes after she had stopped talking to Jeanne.

This is what I needed, she thought, as, fifteen minutes after that, she walked into her sister's home and was quickly gathered in a comforting embrace by her grandmother.

Several hours later Lauren collapsed onto the couch, kicked off her sandals, and rested her feet on the armrest with a sigh of satisfaction. She felt tremendously better than she had that morning.

There'd been only one embarrassing moment in the day, and that was when her grandmother asked her if she and Colby had enjoyed their evening in San Francisco. With cynical amusement Lauren thought that Donnie had purposely turned his pet frog loose on his sister's lap to sway the attention away from her. And it had worked. By the time Jill's screaming had quieted and the grown-ups had returned to their conversation, she and Colby were not the main topic of discussion.

Another of her business lines rang, and Lauren chose to ignore it. It was Sunday, after all, she told herself as she left the couch.

Off and on during the rest of that day and evening, one or more of her business lines would ring, but her own personal line was almost obnoxiously quiet. By the time she was getting ready to go to bed, Lauren would have almost wished that the harassment caller would call on her personal line just to let her know that it was in full operation.

Thankfully, her outrageous wish didn't come true—at least until early Tuesday afternoon—as the caller gave her a two-day respite.

Lauren was sitting at her desk, debating whether or not to call Colby on the pretext of giving him her new number. She suspected he already had it, but she was willing to use it as an excuse to get in touch with him. Just as her hand touched the phone, it rang.

Trembling with a feeling of inevitability, Lauren lifted the receiver to her ear and heard the first in a long line of sexual threats.

How? she wondered, tears streaming down her cheeks. How had the miserable creep learned her new number? Sniffling loudly, she dialed the police station, and when Gordon Hanson answered, she didn't even bother asking to speak with Colby.

She merely said, "This is Lauren Shayler. Tell your lieutenant that the new number didn't do the trick."

"Wait, miss," she heard the sergeant saying, but Lauren hung up the phone.

It rang again almost immediately, but Lauren ignored it, suspecting it would be the smutty talker again. Instead she lowered her tear-stained face to her crossed arms on the desk and for the next few minutes allowed herself the luxury of wallowing in self-pity.

When a knock sounded on the door, Lauren jumped, startled, and was immediately flooded with fear. If the caller could discover her new number so rapidly, even if it was unlisted, then he probably had always known where she lived, and it was only a matter of time before he came over to make good his threats.

And then, "Open the door, Lauren!" penetrated her fear-frozen state.

Colby!

Lauren moved toward the front door as fast as her stiff legs could carry her. She flung open the door and threw herself into his arms with a little sob she couldn't hold back.

"Hey, what's this?" he demanded, surprised, concerned, frightened. He tipped her face up and saw that she had been crying. "The caller?"

She nodded, sniffling loudly. "Oh, Colby, he said such horrible things!"

He half carried, half led her to the couch and then sat

down beside her. "I know you're upset, Lauren, but you're going to have to tell me about it. Are you up to it?"

She licked her lips nervously. "He's gone past making crude suggestions, Colby," she said, her voice strangely quiet. "He's making threats now."

"What kind of threats?"

Little by little Lauren dragged out every abusive word, every insult, every threat, the creep had spoken. And when she was finished, instead of taking her into his arms as she had expected, Colby muttered something unintelligible under his breath and left the couch.

"I'd like to be here the next time he calls."

"To do what?" Remembering that the last time he had asked her to invite the scum into her home, Lauren stiffened her spine and went on, if a little shakily. "He knows when you try to set a trap for him. As long as he's safely at the other end of the line, he's sacrosanct."

"Thanks for the vote of confidence," he snapped.

A downward sweep of her long lashes veiled the humiliation that darkened her eyes. She hadn't meant to make him feel inadequate.

"I'm sorry, Colby," she whispered sorrowfully. "I hate what's happening to me. I guess I'm so filled with anger I can't see who it is that I'm striking out at. I don't like being a victim, dammit!"

Anger was preferable to the fear, the self-pity, she had exhibited earlier. But he didn't want it directed at him. Colby smiled faintly as he lowered himself down to the couch again.

"Lord, Lauren, do you think I want to see you victimized?" He made a move to take her hand, thought better of it, and left the couch again. He would be better off pacing.

"That's why I want to be here the next time he calls." Anger directed at the culprit who was making her so miserable made the expression in his eyes flint-hard. He knew that only someone intimately acquainted with her would have

138

access to her new number, or to those belonging to the businesses that used her service. But who could it be? he wondered. The woman knew too many damn people!

Lauren hadn't missed a single blink of his tawny eyes, or any of the frowns that skittered across his wide forehead. A gut feeling told her that he knew something he wasn't going to tell her even if she questioned him about it.

"All right," she said with a sigh, and left the couch. "I'll do whatever you suggest."

If only you were this amenable all the time, he thought with a wicked smile. "I'd like to stay the night," he said, "and then tomorrow I want to call the phone company and have them put a tracer on your line." His smile was apologetic. "I'm sorry we cannot do more at the moment, but I think the tracer on your personal line will be all you'll need."

"I hope so," she replied, glancing at the switchboard. If the miserable man had to call her at all, she hoped he would call on her personal line. "You can stay in the extra bedroom."

"Don't go to any trouble," Colby said quickly. "I can sleep here on the couch, if you don't mind." He glanced meaningfully toward the phone. "That way I would be right on hand when—if he calls again."

Lauren knew she would feel more comfortable with him in the bedroom. Ever since she had started getting those blasted calls, she had not slept well. When she was too restless even to stay in bed she liked to come out into the living room to read, or to work on her business ledgers.

"Oh, I couldn't ask you to sleep on the couch," she scoffed. "Not when I have a perfectly good guest room with a bed that's big enough even for you." She gave him a swift up-and-down glance. "The couch happens to be barely five feet long."

Colby gave in with good grace. "All right, since you insist. I just didn't want to put you to any extra trouble."

"No trouble at all." *As long as we don't count the sleepless hours I'll have to cope with having you in the next room.*

Famous last words, he thought grimly. "I'll just go out and get the tape recorder."

Lauren watched him moving toward the door, and it struck her that he was nearly jogging. Charging his haste to a desire to get started with his surveillance, she shrugged it off and went into the guest room to put clean sheets on the bed.

"I have to go to my apartment to pick up a couple of things," Colby said as she joined him several minutes later in the living room. "And just so that you won't be surprised if someone calls here for me, I'm leaving word at the station that I'll be here in case they need me."

"I understand." Lauren glanced at the apparatus sitting on her desk. It looked like no tape recorder she had ever seen, and took up most of her work area.

Watching her, Colby explained, "Voices are as unique as fingerprints. With this baby we'll get the caller dead to rights."

Provided, of course, that the miserable man could be caught and his voice compared to the one Colby was so eager to tape. "You'll forgive me if I don't get down on my knees to pay homage to it, won't you?" she remarked, afraid to hope that the end of the harassment calls was imminent.

For a moment Colby just stared at her as though she had suddenly sprouted horns. And then he swore. *For two cents . . .* he thought. Swallowing back another expletive, he said softly, "Will you be all right if I leave you alone while I go to my apartment for my things?"

"I'll be fine," she murmured, disappointed he had not asked her to go with him, but determined not to show it.

He smiled warmly. "How about if I stop somewhere, get something to make for dinner?"

"Can you cook?"

"Can't you?"

"Of course I can. But you sounded as though you were going to cook dinner for me." She smiled mischievously. "I was going to let you."

"I see. You think I can't cook."

"Can you?"

"Prepare your palate for one of the most delicious crab soufflés this side of anywhere!"

"I can hardly wait." The tip of her tongue made a full circle around her mouth, and then she smacked her lips. "And it had better not be Mrs. Paul's!" she threatened.

Laughing, shaking his head at her outrageousness, Colby left to go to the station, promising that he would return by six o'clock.

But six o'clock came without even a phone call from him. Lauren went to the phone, with the idea of calling the police station to ask if he was still there, and then remembered that he was also going to his apartment.

I'll give him until seven o'clock, she thought, *and then I'm going to start dinner for myself.*

It was seven-fifteen, and still there was no word from Colby. Lauren felt a funny, sinking sensation in the pit of her stomach that had nothing to do with hunger. She called the Time of Day service, hoping to discover that all the timepieces in her house were running fast by a whole hour. But the nasal voice declared that at the tone, the time would be seven-fifteen and thirty seconds.

Her stomach grumbled protestingly, reminding Lauren that she'd had nothing to eat since having brunch with her family. She wouldn't wait any longer, she decided, and went into the kitchen. She threw a small steak into the broiler, made a small salad, and brewed a pot of tea.

Forty-five minutes later, as she was enjoying her second cup of tea and an old Dick Powell mystery, she heard the sounds of a car coming to a stop in her driveway.

Relief flowed through her and right on its wake came a rush of anger.

You took your own sweet time! she thought as she went to the door. Perversely, she waited until she heard his knock, and then counted to ten before opening the door.

"Tell me," she said frigidly, "did it take you very long to catch our dinner? Were the silly little things too elusive for you?"

A sheepish smile played over his mouth as Colby stood there with a small flight bag in one hand and a pale-yellow rose in the other. "Would you believe that I went to three different stores looking for fresh crab for our soufflé, but they were all out?"

Lauren couldn't help but smile at the little-boy expression on his face. "I take it that rose is by way of an apology?"

"Actually, I thought I could bribe you with it. You see, I'm hungry, and my pantry and refrigerator were as bare as old Mother Hubbard's."

"Come on in," she said, sighing heavily, dramatically, as she turned away. "I'll fix you something."

"Bless your compassionate heart," he murmured, too low for her to hear.

CHAPTER TEN

"Damn!" The word resounded eerily in the quiet room and returned to taunt him. Colby gritted his teeth, and for the third time since he'd come to bed, he slammed his fist into the center of the pillow, blaming it for his restlessness.

He groaned aloud and buried his face into the pillow. Why hadn't he just told her to get her number changed again? He wished he could get up, get dressed, and then get the hell back to his own apartment. That wouldn't keep Lauren from waltzing in and out of his thoughts at will, but having her just a few yards away and knowing he couldn't touch her was sheer torment.

A crunching sound, like a footstep tramping down the fallen leaves, arrested his unhappy thoughts in midstream. Instinctively, he stiffened, straining to hear, taxing his brain to define the other sounds that seemed to be coming from somewhere between his bedroom and Lauren's.

Holding himself rigid, hardly daring to breathe, he slid out of bed and slipped into his slacks as he crept barefoot out of the bedroom. He couldn't risk turning on any lights, or making any noise that would arouse Lauren from what was probably her first sound sleep in weeks, so he had to depend on his memory to keep him from bumping into any furniture.

There was a door that led from the kitchen to the garage, and as with most garages, a side door would give him access to the backyard. Colby smiled fiendishly. He would circle

143

around, come up behind the intruder before he could get away. Moving solely on instinct, he headed unerringly toward the kitchen and gained the outside without making a sound.

The restless nights she'd had to endure lately had taken their toll. Lauren slept, her body curved around the second pillow, her own pillow long abandoned and lying on the floor.

A crashing sound jarred her out of her dreams. Lauren was instantly awake, her keen senses alert, her body primed for flight. Even as her heart pounded in fear, her eyes were peering through the darkness, swiftly scanning the room, dreading to find an intruder ready to lunge at her. But there was no one.

What was going on? What had awakened her? Taking courage from having Colby sleeping in the next room, she decided to investigate. She moved quietly through the dark but familiar house, grabbing a papier-mâché soldier as she went into the living room. Someone had given it to her to use as a doorstop, but tonight it would have to serve as a weapon. Granted, it wasn't much, but it would have to do.

She remembered having bolted the front door before going to bed, but suddenly she wasn't sure whether or not she had secured the kitchen door. Caught between being afraid of putting herself in jeopardy by going into the kitchen and knowing that she must secure the door, Lauren hesitated by the switchboard. Wanting to run back to the comparative safety of her bedroom, yet knowing she mustn't, she went into the kitchen and immediately to the back door. Just as she had feared, the door was ajar.

And someone was coming through it!

She would never know why she didn't turn on her heel and run for dear life, but as the intruder stepped inside the room, she swung at his midsection with all the power she could muster. She caught the would-be burglar off his guard and staggered him.

With an "Ooomph!" and flailing arms that found nothing to hang on to, the big man started down. Lauren stepped back out of his way and switched on the light to see who it was she had nailed.

Colby?

The expression on his face as he was going down was absolutely priceless. Lauren tried not to laugh—he really wouldn't appreciate her humor—but she was unable to control the nervous fit of giggles that overwhelmed her.

Colby had had the wind knocked from out of him before, but never before by a featherweight. He'd broken his fall with his hands, so the only injury was to his pride. Her hilarity didn't help, either, he thought, sneaking a scowling look up at Lauren. She had one arm hugging her stomach as though it hurt—and it probably did—and a hand at her mouth, trying to quiet her laughter. But it was futile. Her shoulders—her entire body, in fact—shook with laughter.

And what a body! He looked his fill, following the line of her slender body avidly, thirstily drinking in the gentle sloping of her firm young breasts, the curving in of her slim waist, the nicely rounded hips. Dressed in a frilly little nothing of a black gown with scalloped hem that barely reached to mid-thigh, her sleep-tumbled blond hair shimmering under the light, Lauren was sensuality personified.

He found himself aching for her and, in view of the humiliation he was suffering at her hands, getting angry with himself for his weakness.

"You're really getting a kick out of this, aren't you?" he demanded grumpily, propping himself up on one elbow and turning on his side to conceal his very obvious arousal.

Lauren pursed her lips in an attempt to stifle her amusement, but it was no use. "If you could've seen your expression, you'd be laughing too," she sputtered in self-defense, gulping in air between words as though her lungs were starving for oxygen.

He couldn't stay angry with her. "For a little twerp, you sure pack a mean wallop," he growled as he scrambled to his feet. Lauren noticed a pinkish sort of bruise that ran along his midsection, which coincidentally matched the shape of the soldier's back.

"You should warn a person when you're going to be out there skulking around," she retorted, choking back a laugh. He didn't seem angry anymore, but he wasn't smiling either.

"I wasn't skulking!"

She lifted one shoulder in a shrug. "You coulda fooled me."

He took a step forward, and she took one back.

"Are you afraid of me, Laurie?" he taunted in a soft, velvety voice. He moved closer and smiled with wicked amusement as she backed up another step.

Laurie?

"Should I be?" Another backward step brought her up against the refrigerator. Lauren started as her skin came in contact with the cold chrome handle. Nervously, she toyed with the soldier, the movement catching his attention.

"Brandishing your weapon as a warning?" He slanted a withering look down at her hand and was distracted by the perfectly etched features, the detail put into the Union soldier's bright blue uniform.

Lauren swallowed, hard. "Effective, isn't it?" she jeered softly as she looked down at her "weapon." The soldier was eighteen inches long and heavy enough to stun a man as big as Colby. Granted, she had caught him by surprise, but she had knocked the wind out of him.

He reached down for it and she pulled it back. He laughed softly. "I should think that you'd be more concerned about protecting your *virtue*," he remarked, slipping two fingers under the thin strap that lay across her right shoulder, tugging at it. "I've gotta tell you. That child's toy isn't proof against a man when he's as determined as I am now."

Oh, oh! Lauren cleared her throat nervously. In her haste to get to the kitchen door to secure it against the alleged intruder, she had forgotten her robe. The way Colby was looking at her, she wished she'd remembered to put it on.

She tried to brazen her way out. "You're too much of a gentleman to take advantage of our, uh, situation."

"I am?" One eyebrow skidded upward, and his mouth turned up at the corners.

"Aren't you?" she demanded shakily.

He shrugged. "I guess I'm both," he murmured, closing in on her. "I *am* a man, and I *am* gentle. *Very, very gentle.*" His arms slipped around her body, drawing her inexorably to him. His head descended slowly, his mouth tenderly joined the warmth and sweetness of hers.

Fleetingly, Lauren wondered what she ought to do with the soldier, and then all thought fled, for his caresses were sending tiny electric shocks skittering through her entire body. Between soft, devastating little kisses, he told her how beautiful she was, how much he desired her. Slowly, his lips moved from one sensitive corner of her mouth across to the other, the tip of his tongue teasing and tantalizing until Lauren felt as if she were just a mass of tingling, shivering nerve ends.

He tugged at the straps and, encountering no resistance, slowly slipped them off her shoulders, sliding them down her arms, making her skin tingle as his fingers lightly raked her arm. Holding her away from him, he eased the gown off her and allowed it to fall to the floor.

Lauren stood motionless, her feet lost in the puff of black chiffon, her languid eyes raised to him as he stepped back to view her.

"God, but you're beautiful." Hands that were eager to lose themselves in the silken warmth of her body settled on her shoulders, with gentle insistence drawing her to him. He held her while his mouth claimed hers again, more insistently than before, exploring the moist, honeyed cavern in a thrillingly urgent sort of way.

Lauren trembled when her breasts brushed against the pleasant roughness of the forest of crisp hair that covered his chest. She pressed closer, urgently seeking release of the gnawing ache that was spreading across her lower abdomen and thighs. Her hands slipped between them, gliding over his chest, exhilaration coursing through her when she felt him shudder under her touch.

"Ahhhh," was whispered across her shoulder, and then he buried his face in the silken tumble of her hair, exigent hands roughly sliding over the smooth curve of her hips. With a groan he lifted her into his arms. Between the kitchen and the bedroom he told her he loved her body, her hair, the way she smiled, her husky voice. Catching her lower lip between his teeth, he murmured that she made him feel like a young boy with his first girl.

"You can remember that far back?" she teased, her voice a breathless whisper.

He laughed, gathering her to him, kissing her long and hard as he climbed up on her bed with her still cradled against his chest. As though he were afraid to hurt her, or reluctant to part with her, he very slowly lowered her to the center of the bed and then stretched his body alongside hers.

"I love you, Colby," she confessed, smoothing her fingers across his forehead, running them teasingly down the side of his cheek while her eyes watched for his reaction.

Something flickered in his eyes, something that sent a flash of apprehension shooting down to the tips of her toes. Bewildered, fearful, Lauren scanned his features, her confusion intensifying when she noticed the rueful expression in his eyes.

"Before we go any farther, there's something that I must tell you, Lauren."

She swallowed. "You have a wife hidden somewhere, and five kids."

His smile lacked humor, warmth. "Nothing quite that drastic. But you have to know about Anne."

Lauren caught her breath, expelled it slowly. She hadn't expected this. And, suddenly, she was afraid. She didn't want to know, about Anne, about the redhead at the Dandy Diner, about the faceless women who might be littering his past. Hiding an inexplicable feeling of inadequacy behind a swiftly erected wall of anger, she muttered, "Your timing's not the greatest. Why the hell did you wait until now to tell me about your darling Anne?"

At first startled by her outrage, he suddenly laughed. "She's not my darling Anne, my darling anything, baby." He studied her with eyes that were soft with love, as warm as the line of his mouth. "I've never said 'I love you' to any other woman, and before I can say it to you, I have to explain something about Anne."

"So, explain!" She closed her eyes against a miserable stab of jealousy so devastating she cringed under its force. What was she doing? Why didn't she just order him to leave her bed? *Because I love him.*

As he made his explanation, the only emotion that she heard in his voice was regret, regret that the year-long affair he had had with Anne Mulrooney had ended on a sour note. It bothered him that Anne might be harboring ill feelings toward him, and all he wanted from Lauren was her understanding. He must see Anne again. He couldn't make a commitment to Lauren feeling that Anne Mulrooney was a loose end. He hated loose ends.

"I wanted you to know so that if ever you hear that I was seen in her company, you will understand why I had to see her one more time."

Was that all? Lauren opened her eyes wide, searched his features, and was overwhelmed with a longing to be close to him, to become one with him.

149

He would never know what it cost her to say, "See her again if you must, Colby."

Colby gathered her to him, grateful that she understood, happy because trust in a relationship was very important to him and she was giving it to him along with her love. Dropping soft, tiny kisses all over her face, he studied her body with his hands, slowly, deftly fevering her skin until it seemed she had liquid fire coursing through her veins.

He moved away from her a moment to divest himself of his slacks, and he flung them carelessly down to the floor.

A mouth that was sweet and tender touched the hollow of her cheek, brushed across her forehead, down the line of her small nose. Long, strong fingers weaved into her hair, relishing its silkiness, bringing it to his mouth. Moaning softly, Lauren curled her arms tightly around his neck, holding his head while her mouth joined his, opening to invite the exploration of his tongue. Tongues teased, held, caressed.

His fingers blazed a fiery trail down the length of her body, lingering in the cloud of curly blond hair that crowned her womanhood. He urged her thighs apart and fondled her in a way that was exquisite torture for Lauren. She arched her body into his hand, moaning softly at the waves of pleasure that radiated outward from her abdomen. He continued to caress her, to drive her, Lauren feared, to the brink of madness with desire.

"Colby, please, I don't think I can take any more," she moaned.

His mouth almost touching her ear, he whispered, "I love you, Laurie," as he moved his body over hers. "God, how I love you."

"I love you," she breathed through smiling lips, and parted her thighs to him.

Colby plunged all of himself deep inside, and burrowed farther. When he heard her sharp intake of breath, he stilled. Until this moment he had never thought that celibacy over a long period of time could make a woman seem like a virgin again, that she could feel pain at penetration. And he remembered that he was, thankfully, well-endowed.

"Are you all right?" he whispered, concerned.

She swallowed. "I will be, in a second."

When the pain had subsided, Lauren subtly moved under him, sending a shaft of sensation spiraling through him that left his body shaking. Colby hugged Lauren and began to rock over her, increasing momentum as she started to move with him.

"My God!" he cried, shaken by the exquisite pleasure that saturated his mind, his heart, his manhood warmly sheathed inside her.

Breathless, shuddering, Lauren clung to him as the rhythm of their primitive dance of love intensified. She felt as if they were caught on a storm-ravaged sea, being swept away on a wave that never broke on the far-distant shore. His mouth swallowed the tiny sob that heralded her climax, and he held her close, loving her with soothing words and warm caresses until her trembling had subsided.

And then, slowly, he began to move again, holding her fast against his deep, almost frantic thrusts, until he couldn't control the shudder that tore through his body any more than he could control the burst of fire that exploded from his loins.

Afterwards, they lay side by side, their hands clasped between their heated bodies.

"I love being with you," Colby whispered, nuzzling her shoulder with his nose.

"Then, stay," she murmured, snuggling into him, draping a slender leg across his thighs.

"Forever," he promised, gathering her to him closely, dropping a kiss on her mouth to seal the promise.

"Colby?" she murmured a long moment later, and he made a noncommittal sound. "What were you doing outside?"

"I thought I'd heard a prowler," he murmured sleepily, "but it was only my imagination working overtime."

"Mmmm." She snuggled closer and, dropping a tantalizingly soft kiss on the nipple closer to her mouth, closed her eyes and went to sleep.

He woke her again just when dawn was pinking the edges of the sky, opalescent light dancing into the room through the tall, narrow windows on either side of the bed.

And long after their hungers had been sated, he raised himself up on one elbow and looked at her.

"A man could get used to this," he said, running a finger across her smiling mouth.

So could a woman, Lauren discovered in the next three days. Colby went to work and came home to her each evening, and to her bed each night. Lauren convinced herself that she had finally found the perfect happiness. She had everything, a job she enjoyed and the love of a man who had suddenly become the most important person in her life.

That Friday, as they were enjoying a glass of wine after a delicious dinner they had prepared together, Colby leaned back in his chair and for a long, tense moment sat staring into the dark-red liquid in his wineglass.

He appeared to be brooding about something, and immediately Lauren felt the muscles of her stomach tightening with apprehension. She looked at the plates on the table, at the half-full carafe of wine, at the bread basket, and finally, inevitably, she lifted a quizzical gaze to his face.

"Is something wrong?" She had to know. No matter what it was, or how bad, she had to know. *Please, please tell me,* she begged silently. *Don't shut me out.*

"What?" He looked up, and she noticed there was a remote expression in his eyes, as though he had been mentally miles away and had had to force himself back to her. "I'm sorry." His smile was rueful. "I was just wondering how to tell you something you're not going to enjoy hearing."

Her heart quaked in fear. Had he seen Anne Mulrooney

again and was he having difficulty telling her that their love affair had been just a pleasant interlude? She steeled herself to hear the worst. "You've been very honest and direct with me so far," she said, curling her hands into fists under the table. "Don't change now."

"It was your nephew all the time," he said finally, setting his wineglass down on the table with a heavy, weary sigh. "Donald Ryan Hunter." There was anger underlying his quiet tone.

"Donnie?" she asked, shocked, blinking in confusion. "What has Donnie got to do with anything? With us?"

"He's your caller. The phone company traced all the calls to the Hunter number."

"I can't believe it!" Lauren said, clenching her back teeth until her jaw ached. But the more she thought about it, the more likely it seemed. With hindsight she recalled the interest he had shown in the switchboard, the way he had tested his memory of the businesses that used the Speedy Answering Service. It was no wonder the calls had started again, despite the new number.

"Oooh, I could kill him!" she exploded, filled with righteous indignation.

"In that case I might end up arresting you for mass murder," Colby teased, a faint smile warming the gold in his eyes. "You see, love, there are two other young culprits. Buddies of Donnie who had nothing better to do with their spare time, so they joined in Donnie's fun."

She hadn't detected any differences in the caller's voice at any time. Perhaps it was because she had not been listening to the sound of the voice so much as to what the miserable brats had been saying.

"Where are you going?" he asked as Lauren pushed away from the table and started moving toward the door.

"To call Jeanne. You don't think I'm going to let Donnie get away with this, do you?" She gritted her teeth and breathed in deeply, to quiet her anger. After all, it wasn't

Colby's fault that Donnie had been tormenting her for weeks. "And if she won't do anything about it, I'll tell Rob about it and then take great delight in seeing him nail that little brat's hide to the wall."

"I'm sorry, baby, but it's not up to you to see that Donnie and his friends are punished." His hand snaked out, curled around her wrist, held her, as Lauren tried to walk past him. "Sit down, Lauren. Let me tell you what *is* going to be done about them."

Lauren felt a serpent of fear twining in the pit of her stomach. "What are you going to do to him?" she demanded fearfully, struggling to free her arm.

His eyes opened wide with surprise. "Calm down. I'm not going to take him out and use him for target practice." It would be all right if *she* took the boy and boiled him in oil, as long as no one else touched him. He shook his head in amazement. This was not the first—nor would it be the last —time he had seen this reaction.

"It became a police matter the day you made your complaint, Lauren," he said gently, and, pulling her down, settled her on his lap and wrapped his arms around her. "I know you don't like it, but you're going to have to stay out of it from now on."

She couldn't do that, and he should know better than to ask her to. "What are you going to do?"

"I'm going to have to gather the offenders together with their parents and—"

"Oh, no!" She turned sharply to him, looking panicked. "Couldn't you just have a private talk with Jeanne and Rob, sort of 'off the record'?" At the moment she could think no further than saving her sister and brother-in-law the humiliation of having the police come to their house to question their son.

Colby shook his head. "He has broken the law, Lauren. He has to face the music."

He was adamant. Lauren argued, pleaded, cajoled, but

154

Colby was unmoving. The boys had committed an offense, and they should be made responsible for their actions.

Quietly desperate, Lauren offered a compromise. "Do me this one favor, please, Colby, and I'll never ask you for another." When he tried to talk, she pressed her fingers to his mouth, silencing him.

"I'm not asking you to ignore what Donnie and his friends have done. What I *am* asking is for you to meet with Rob and Jeanne in private, to give them a chance to prepare themselves for the embarrassment. I'm thinking only of what this will do to Rob. He is a city councilman." A frown puckered the skin just above her nose. Jeanne was going to be hurt no matter what happened, but if Lauren could save Rob public discomfort, she would do everything in her power to do it.

"Are you asking me to meet with the other parents in private also?" He sounded doubtful.

"Of course!"

Seeing how determined she was, Colby grudgingly agreed. "You win. I'll do it. You can call your sister and make an appointment for me to see them both."

That sounded too cold. "I'll ask Jeanne and Rob to dinner with us Saturday night, all right?"

He nodded. "And now, I have to go make a couple of phone calls of my own."

Lauren sensed his withdrawal even before he pushed her off his lap. She watched him leaving the kitchen, confused. She hadn't expected him to be jumping with joy, but it wasn't as though she had asked him to compromise his ethics, either!

Abruptly, she turned around and busied herself with clearing the table, with doing the dishes, with shining the chrome of her appliances, until her arm felt leaden from the exertion. Anything to keep herself from going to the living room until Colby had finished with his calls.

CHAPTER ELEVEN

"Oh, how could they!" Jeanne cried brokenly. Tears had lurked in the corners of her large green eyes while she had sat in disbelieving silence listening to what Colby was saying. Now they trailed slowly, unheeded, down her cheeks, to gather unnoticed in the corners of her mouth.

They were sitting around the kitchen table, Rob and Lauren on one side, with Jeanne and Colby facing them. Colby had waited until the dishes had been cleared away and the four were enjoying a second bottle of wine before bringing up the most unpleasant subject of Donnie's obscene calls.

"Damn those kids!" Rob muttered with a furious shake of his head. When he looked across at Colby, Lauren noticed that there was a pulse going wild along Rob's jawline. "Pick them all up, take them to the station, put the fear of God into them." His eyes brooded, but his voice was so deadly calm, it raised shivers on Lauren's neck and arms. "It'll give them something to think about the next time they get it into their twisted little minds to pull another hurtful stunt like this."

Lauren simply couldn't believe what she was witnessing. She glanced over at Jeanne, expecting her to jump to Donnie's defense as she had done so many times before, but her sister was almost mulishly silent. Turning again to Rob, she cringed. She had never seen this man look so terrifying before. His murderous expression boded ill for his son.

She should have been deliriously happy to know that

156

Donnie was finally going to get a royal comeuppance, but somehow she didn't feel like rejoicing. She was confused by emotions she hadn't expected to feel when her tormentor was finally nailed. She felt a strange sort of sympathy for the boy, mingled with a dash of pity and a totally illogical desire to defend him.

Quick to notice the sorrowful look in Lauren's expressive eyes, Colby reached across the table and patted her hand. There was a wealth of love and understanding in his warm touch, but a decidedly wicked glint of amusement in his tawny eyes. "Don't look so worried, love. I'm not going to hurt them very much, really. I already got my jollies for the week, anyway," he added, leaning back in his chair, clasping his large hands behind his head. He laughed softly, and added, "I busted two little old ladies who were racing stolen shopping carts around Dublin, so I've put my rubber hose and cattle prod away for the time being."

They all laughed with him, but Lauren noticed that Rob's laughter was forced. It was understandable that he did not feel very jovial. He was hurt, embarrassed, disappointed. Her heart went out to him, and her own anger toward Donnie resurfaced. The little monster had tormented her, caused her many sleepless nights, made her afraid to even answer the phone, and nearly destroyed her self-confidence, but all of that was nothing compared to the hurt he had inflicted on his father.

"Why do they do it?" Rob's voice was flat, defeated, his eyes lackluster.

Colby shrugged. "All sorts of reasons that seem very legitimate to them." There was a contemplative look in his eyes as he focused them on Lauren. "In your son's case it's that he resents Lauren, I'm sorry to say."

Jeanne looked appalled, but Rob seemed to understand. "I've suspected that for a while."

"Why should he resent her?" Jeanne demanded, almost glaring at her husband. A hand fluttered to her chest, her

157

fingers nervously played with the lace edging on the collar of her brown silk blouse as Rob leveled a cold, hard look at her.

Colby answered. "I believe it's because she's very special to you and Rob."

Jeanne looked bewildered, pained. "So is Tish, but he's never done anything to hurt her."

Colby hadn't yet been introduced to Tish. But Rob knew her almost too well. "It's not the same with Tish," he mumbled. "Laurie's special in a different way. You mothered her for years, and I . . ." His eyes sought Lauren's, warm with love. "I have always thought her the icing on the cake."

Lauren beamed. She felt the same love for him. She smiled, remembering how she had practiced her flirting on him as a teen, and then later plagued him with her attentions when she had, briefly, been infatuated with him. Now they enjoyed a beautiful camaraderie.

A sharp, unexpected stab of jealousy made Colby wince inwardly. *Hell!* he thought, disgusted with himself. *What are you thinking? The councilman's in love with his own wife, for goodness' sakes!* But the feeling persisted, and before it could consume him, he pushed himself away from the table and rose quickly to his feet.

"Sat long enough, huh?" Lauren remarked. During the past three days she had learned several things about him, one of which was that he couldn't sit for very long. He was too restless.

He glanced pointedly at his watch. "I'm sorry, babe. I came home early to be on time for dinner with you all, so I left a few reports to do later. And it's 'later' now, so I have to get back." He stretched a glance between Rob and Jeanne. "I'll be in touch with you very soon about your son." He said good-bye and left the room.

"I'll be right back," Lauren whispered, jumping to her feet, rushing after him.

"Will you be very late?" she asked as she caught up to him at the door.

He turned slowly and smiled. "I'll try not to be."

She raised her face for his kiss, and when his lips brushed her temple, her closed lids, her mouth, she felt a stirring of desire. She moved closer, clinging to him, boldly using her body to make him forget the reports waiting for him.

"Save my place," he said, holding her away. "And keep the hearth fires burning."

Lauren laughed. She was disappointed that he was leaving, but happy because she knew he would sail through his work and hurry home to her.

Jeanne and Rob left soon after that, and Lauren wandered aimlessly through the house, wondering why it suddenly felt so huge, so empty, so lonely. When she found herself going to the kitchen window for the third time, hoping to find Colby's shiny black car coming onto her driveway, she knew she had to do something to occupy her hands, if not her mind.

With single-minded purpose she went to the hall closet, dragged out the vacuum cleaner, and went through the entire house with it, manually picking up everything the machine couldn't, even the tiniest ball of lint. When she finally returned the vacuum to the closet, the carpet that covered over three quarters of her home was cleaner than it had been in weeks.

Still restless, Lauren changed into her sweats and went jogging, hoping that the exercise would make her too tired to fret.

An hour later she returned to the house, her breath coming in short, ragged gasps, her face beaded with perspiration, her bangs damp and clinging to her cheeks. She went immediately to the bathroom, stripped, and then stepped under a comfortably hot shower. She washed her hair, shaved her legs, and toyed with the idea of giving her hair a hot-oil treatment, just to pass the time.

But it would be like Colby to show up while she had a plastic bag over her head, she thought. It was enough to send her to the vanity to dry her hair.

Wearing only her robe, Lauren sat on the wrought iron bench. With the dryer poised over her head, she stared into her reflection, feeling somewhat detached as she took in the unhappy expression of her image, the downward curve on the mouth, the mournful look in the green eyes.

It was true. She was unhappy. Here it was Saturday night, still early, and she was alone. And lonely.

Lauren couldn't remember ever having felt so lonely. She liked being alone, sought other company only when she was in the mood for it, and spent enough time with her family so that she didn't feel apart from them. Since leaving college she had gone out with a few carefully selected males. She had been propositioned by most, proposed to by some, but she'd been celibate, by choice, since her affair with Johnny Tolan. And she had never been lonely.

Until now.

Please, please, come home right now, she thought, wishing fervently for the power to teleport her thoughts, her wishes, her desires, to the man she so desperately needed.

But he didn't come. The clock ticked away the minutes, the hours, but there was no car coming to a stop in her driveway, no soft footfalls approaching her bedroom. After waiting what seemed an eternity, Lauren went to bed and cried herself to sleep, something she hadn't done since she'd walked out on Johnny Tolan.

She woke the next morning to the sound of rain pounding on her roof and splattering against her windows. She smiled sleepily and turned, hoping to find Colby sleeping beside her.

I wonder if he came home at all, she thought, staring with misty eyes at the side of the bed that hadn't been slept on.

And then she heard a noise coming from the direction of the kitchen. She sat up quickly and reached for her robe. Slipping it on as she went, she dashed into the bathroom, rinsed her mouth, ran a comb through her hair, and then hurried into the kitchen, slowing herself to a sedate walk as she reached the door.

The most delicious aromas greeted her as she stepped into the kitchen. Colby was at the stove, a dish towel tied at his waist serving as an apron. There was coffee brewing, and a few slices of toast waited to be buttered in a plate near the coffee maker.

A fluttering excitement agitated her pulses when Colby turned around to her. "Good morning," she said softly, feeling unaccountably insecure.

"Mornin'." Colby held his breath, his eyes studying, with a hunger he couldn't disguise, the sleepy-eyed woman standing so tantalizingly close to him. Her large eyes were cloudy with the remnants of sleep, her mouth soft, enticing.

"Do you have everything you need?" she asked, meaning pots, pans, and the like.

"Now I do," he said, meaning her. "How about a cup of coffee?" He took down two mugs from the cupboard, filled them with the steaming brew, and then motioned her to join him as he set the mugs down on the table.

"How are you this morning?" he asked mildly.

Miserable. Resentment seethed through Lauren, eroding the cool façade she was struggling so hard to project. But "I'm fine," she lied, wrapping the coffee mug in her shaky hands, bringing her concentration to bear on the warmth seeping into her fingers.

"And you?" she murmured, blowing away the steam that rose from the mug to hide the giveaway quiver she felt on her mouth.

"Miserable," he admitted. "I missed you last night."

"Oh?" If she sounded doubtful, she had good reason.

He arched a brow. "Do I detect a hint of doubt in that 'Oh?' "

She shrugged, and lowered her gaze to her mug, dis-

161

tractedly noticing that it needed replenishment. She set it on the table with a thud.

He figured she was upset with him because he had not come to her bed last night. His smile was a trifle smug as he set his mug down to go to her. He would be ecstatically happy to correct his oversight.

When he started walking toward her, Lauren had no idea what he intended, and let out a tiny meow of surprise when he lifted her off the chair in a single, swift movement. He held her tightly to him, apologizing for having abandoned her the previous night, her name an emotion-packed litany on his lips until his mouth merged with hers in a kiss that left them both breathless and shaken.

"Your breakfast?" Lauren reminded him, and he mumbled, "Later," and carried her into the bedroom.

This was to set the pattern of their lives for the next two weeks. Delayed or broken dates. Ruined dinners. Apologies instead of explanations.

And too much loneliness for me, Lauren thought, her eyes suddenly filling with tears. She loved Colby more than she had ever imagined was possible to love a man, but she had sadly reached the conclusion that loving him wasn't enough. For him.

Her throat swelled with emotion as she dialed her parents' number, but when her mother answered, she managed to sound cheerful in inviting herself to their house for dinner. Colby hadn't bothered to tell her when she could expect him home, and she couldn't stand the thought of spending another evening alone.

"Of course you can, darling," Lina Shayler said quickly, her voice soft with compassion. "Gram has made your favorite, cabbage rolls."

"Great! I'll be right over," Lauren said with a laugh, and hung up. She wouldn't have cared if they were having fried liver, which she absolutely detested. At the moment she felt

162

desperate and needed her family to ease away the feeling of inadequacy that had her in its dreadful grip.

Five minutes later she was on her way to Silvergate, to the home of her childhood, an imposing two-story house with a veranda that circled the entire second floor, where she and her sisters had had their bedrooms.

Colby's car was parked in the driveway when she came home some two hours later.

"It figures," Lauren muttered grumpily. "The one night I decide to go out, he's home early."

She parked the car in the garage, and then went into the house through the kitchen. She hesitated for a moment to catch her breath and then hurried into the living room, expecting to find him reading the paper on the couch. But the room was ominously empty.

Ahhh! she thought, smiling. He was probably taking a shower. Dropping her bag on a chair, she crept cautiously toward the bedroom, planning to sneak into the bathroom to surprise him. She might even decide to go into the shower with him, she thought, and then came to a dead stop just inside the bedroom.

"Colby!" Eyes wide with horror, Lauren stared at him, unable to go to him, though she longed to do so. He had no shirt on, and his chest was wrapped in bandages from just under his nipples to his midriff.

"Hey, don't look so scared." His smile was crooked, and as he stretched a hand to her, his features contorted with pain. "Come here," he whispered huskily.

With a small, incoherent cry she was across the room, kneeling on the floor beside the bed.

"Oh, Colby," she cried, "what happened to you?"

His wounds had not affected his sense of humor. "You remember those two little old ladies with the shopping carts?" He laughed, and winced with pain. "Well, they're back, terrorizing the neighborhood again. Like an idiot I

163

took them on again, and look what they did to me." He moaned, and Lauren quickly raised her eyes to his face.

She was not amused. And she was looking. She saw that he grimaced with pain every time he moved or laughed.

"What happened?"

"Promise not to laugh?"

"Do I look like I'm enjoying this?"

"It was my own fault that I got hurt," he started, and went on to tell her that he'd been chasing two kids who'd vandalized one of the plant nurseries. The culprits had abandoned their car on the freeway, and then fled on foot. He had followed, also on foot.

"There I was, doing the four-forty in nothing flat, almost ready to apprehend them, when my big feet caught on an exposed cable, and I went rolling down the embankment." He grimaced with self-disgust. "They got away, and I got a couple of bruised ribs and muscle strain for my efforts."

"You could've been killed," she said, angry with him because he didn't seem inclined to give his situation the proper respect.

"Naw," he countered with a shaky laugh. "If I'd landed on my head, I wouldn't even have to be all trussed up like a Thanksgiving turkey."

Lauren shook her head, despairing of him. She lifted herself tiredly to her feet. "Would you like something to eat?"

"I've eaten already." He curled a weak hand around her arm to detain her as she started away. "I tried to call you, babe, but you weren't home."

"I was having dinner with my folks."

He glanced away from her. "That's what I figured."

Finding herself free to go, Lauren murmured, "I'm going to make a pot of tea," and left the room.

She hurried into the kitchen, sat down, and then dropped her face onto her crossed arms on the table. Although her eyes burned, she was too numb to cry.

In the days that followed, Lauren was almost grateful to the vandals Colby had been chasing when he had his accident. Having him home was a beautiful dream that she never wanted to end.

"So, lovely lady, what's on the agenda for today?" Dressed in black jeans and a blue T-shirt, he stood framed at the kitchen door, looking down at Lauren, who was sitting at the switchboard.

"We're invited to dinner at Jeanne's," she said, then held up her hand to delay his response while she answered one of the lines.

"Would Jeanne mind awfully much if you and I skipped dinner with them tonight?" he asked when he finally had her attention again.

His boyish grin was devastating. Lauren would've risked her entire family's displeasure for a night alone with him, particularly now that his ribs had healed. "If it means having you all to myself all night, I'll risk disappointing her."

"You really don't mind?"

"What?" She laughed softly. "Having you all to myself all night? Positively not!"

"No, twerp. Disappointing your sister and brother-in-law."

"Normally, I would cut off my fingers to the first joint rather than disappoint any member of my family, but when it comes to spending a night with you . . ." She smiled.

He walked forward, lifted her from the chair, and kissed her soundly. "Thank you. I've been waiting a hell of a long time to make love to you again, and I don't think I could sit through a family dinner when my mind would be on the fun we could be having alone."

She smiled up at him. "I've got a great idea. Why don't you go out and get us a couple of steaks, and the makings for a tossed salad while I finish here?"

Colby's grin was happy, charming. "I'll even get us a bottle of Burgundy." Dropping a kiss on her mouth, he forced her down to her chair again. "I'll see you in a little while."

As they worked to prepare the meal that night, Colby told her that he'd been cleared to go back to work. When he noticed that Lauren was not exactly overjoyed with his news, he set down the knife he'd been using to slice the tomatoes, and took her into his arms.

"What's wrong, honey? Are you afraid I'll get hurt again?"

She shook her head slowly. "I guess I just got used to having you all to myself for a while, and I hate to see it end."

"What do you mean, end?" He tilted her face up with two fingers under her chin and looked deeply into her eyes. "You have me, all of me, all to yourself, Lauren. Don't you know that by now?"

Did she? Lauren had her doubts, but she nodded her reply.

She had taken too long to answer. Colby's gaze scanned her features, probing, trying to see beyond the smile he knew was forced, to the thoughts that had put a haunted look in her eyes.

"Something else is bothering you, Lauren. What is it?"

"Only that I'm not going to like having you go back to work." Her voice quavered.

His own voice was very husky. "I'm going to miss you, too." His strong arms secured her to him. "I love you very much, Laurie, and I love being with you," he whispered against her hair. "But as I am not independently wealthy, I must work. My only consolation is that I don't mind working at a job I like."

He released her slowly, reluctantly, and went back to making the salad. With a heavy heart Lauren scored the steaks, pounded freshly ground garlic into the slits, and then literally threw them into the broiler.

During dinner Colby caught her looking pensive enough

times to realize that there was something troubling her, something, he decided, that she was trying very desperately to keep from him.

A baby? His hand froze midway to his mouth, and he treated Lauren to a sharp, scrutinizing look. Could she be pregnant? Was that what she seemed almost afraid to tell him? He opened his mouth, shut it. They'd never discussed having children, and now that he was faced with the possibility that she might be carrying his child, he didn't know what to say.

I'll face that when she finally tells me, he thought, smiling as he slipped a piece of steak, by now cold, into his mouth.

"I'll tell you what, dear heart," he said as they started clearing the table. "After we get these done, I'm going to take you to a movie. We'll sit and neck in the back row, how's that?" He leered outrageously at her, but his antics were a camouflage for the emotions that were raging through him.

"I've got a better idea. We'll just let the dishes wait." She took his hand and led him quietly into the bedroom.

The next morning Lauren woke early, her body still warm from their passionate lovemaking. She smiled dreamily, stretching sinuously, a satisfied kittenish sound rising from her throat. She had fallen asleep with his head lying next to hers on her pillow, his leg draped across her thighs, his arms wrapped securely around her.

"Hello," he murmured drowsily.

"Hello yourself." She raised herself up, kissed his whiskery chin, and wrinkled her nose.

"I know," he groaned. "I have to shave. But you feel so damned good next to me, I hate to get up."

"Then don't. I won't tell on you if you decide to play hookey with me all day."

"Nor would I." He shifted slightly, took his wristwatch from her nightstand, and scowled at the face of it. "Unfortunately, duty calls."

167

"Ignore it," she advised. "Call in sick. Tell them you're suffering a relapse." With a mischievous smile lining her lips she began a slow, provocative exploration of his body with her fingertips. She loved the feel of his skin, but what she loved most was the reaction she was getting as she ran just the very tips of her fingers across his flat belly.

"Minx," he growled, trapping her hand before she could torment him further. "Don't!" he warned when she struggled to free herself. "You'll get hurt."

"You wouldn't hurt me," she stated unequivocably.

"Not intentionally, sweetheart." He used her trapped hand to pull her toward him and gave her a hearty hug. For a few more moments he savored the feel of her body pressed to his, then reluctantly pushed her away. He left the bed, vibrantly aware that she was following his movements with her eyes.

"You make it very difficult for me to do what I have to do," he accused over his shoulder.

When she heard the shower going, Lauren sat up, slinging her bare legs over the side of the bed. For a moment she just sat there, staring through the open bathroom door at the steam that was building up.

"You're a horrible workaholic, Colby Sherman," she mumbled, and smiled ruefully. He had finally told her why his romance with Anne Mulrooney had failed, and now she was learning, firsthand, what Anne must have had to endure being the lieutenant's woman.

And she didn't like it.

And she wasn't going to put up with it.

"The shower's yours," Colby said as he came back out into the bedroom. He was rubbing his wet hair with a towel, while another of her towels was wrapped around his lower body.

"Thank you."

He stopped rubbing his hair. "All right, Lauren, what's

wrong? And don't tell me 'nothing,' because I won't believe you."

She faced him squarely, her eyes mutinously glinting. "I know how eager you are to get to the station, so I won't keep you but a moment. Just long enough for me to find out whether you're planning to work around the clock now that you're back in the saddle, so to speak."

He stared at her with a look that could fry an egg. "So that's it," he said, pulses throbbing at his temples as he tried to suppress his anger. "You're jealous of my job."

"Wrong word, buddy. Resentful. You use your damned job as an excuse to stay away from me."

"That is not true." He flung down the towel, then turned and took up his slacks from the back of one of the two turquoise velvet bedroom chairs. "I like what I do, and I work very hard at it because I live here, and I want to make this community one that we can all take pride in." He was stuffing his shirt into the waist of his slacks as he spoke, and then continued, less heatedly, as he sat down on the edge of the chair to put on his socks and shoes.

"And it's because of hardworking stiffs like me that the city streets are safe for you, your mother, your grandmother, your sisters, and your niece to walk on without fear of muggers, rapists, and murderers."

With her teeth clenched, her fists clenched at her sides, Lauren glared at his downbent head. Damn him, he was trying to make her feel guilty because she wanted to have more time with him!

"You make it sound like the whole community would fall to ruin if you weren't around to keep it in shape," she snapped. "You're not the only man on the force!"

He glared at her through the damp hair that was hanging over his eyes. "You refuse to understand," he said flatly.

"Oh, I understand, all right. If I want to spend more time with you, I'll just place myself in jeopardy and holler, 'Cop!' "

"Now, you're being ridiculous." He stood and went into the bathroom to comb his hair.

"Excuse me," she mumbled as she slipped past him to turn on the faucets in the shower.

"What are you going to be doing today?" His smile was as phony as the interest he was feigning in her activities.

"I'm going to go to dinner at Tish's." She remembered that her sister had invited them both, but she doubted very much that Colby would be joining them. Particularly now.

"Then you won't miss me if I work late," he stated flatly. With that he walked away. Lauren went into the shower with a fatalistic feeling, and tears in her eyes.

CHAPTER TWELVE

The day was sullen and gray, matching Lauren's spirits to perfection. She went through the motions, forcing herself to concentrate on her work, paying careful attention to each call as though her very livelihood depended on that call alone. And she was the essence of professionalism as she passed on the messages to her clients.

Off and on, as the morning moved at a snail's pace, she would slant a pleading look at Freddy, who had remained ominously silent all morning. She worked stubbornly right through lunch, knowing that if she forced herself to eat, she was very likely to toss her cookies.

At two, when her personal line rang, Lauren ran to answer it, praying it would be Colby. But it was only Jeanne, calling to tell her that Tish had postponed having the family to dinner until the following day.

"Mark can't come until tomorrow," she explained. "And you know our sister. She decided the rest of us wouldn't care when she treated us to dinner as long as she did." She laughed softly. "Same old Tish. Every time there's a new man in her life, she becomes an airhead, like the kids say."

"That's fine with me." Lauren actually felt relieved. "But I'm afraid that I'll be the only one coming."

"Colby has to work late again, I take it?"

"You know how it is," Lauren said, forcing a laugh. "He's the head honcho, and they've had to do without him for nearly two weeks. I'm sure they're going to work his fanny off." She frowned. Lies. Lies that by rights should stick in her throat but which instead flowed from her mouth like sweet spring water from a mountain crevice. *Practice makes perfect, so they say,* she thought, her eyes dull with misery.

After she had rung off, in deference to a stomach that was achy with hunger, she went into the kitchen and fixed a light lunch.

At three-thirty, when Maggie came to relieve her, Lauren met her at the door, her bag slung over her shoulder, the car keys in her hand.

"I might not be back when it's time for you to go home, so just go ahead, but lock up for me, please?"

Maggie grinned impishly. "I think I'll bring a moving van in and make off with everything that isn't nailed down," she teased. "And then, why bother locking the house?"

Throwing a glance around the room, Lauren nodded. "Make sure you start with the switchboard and Freddy," she teased back. "Today, those are two things I can definitely live without."

Maggie's amusement vanished. "Have you been getting more of those stupid calls?" Two little lines of worry appeared between her eyebrows.

"No. The culprit's already been caught." With that, Lauren left, her mood bluer than before. If not for those damned phone calls—Stop! She couldn't—wouldn't—hop aboard that old "If only" merry-go-round.

Even as a child, when she felt at odds with herself, she would go window-shopping, and that would put her to rights after a couple of hours. The way she felt today, it would take a wildly excessive shopping spree to restore her good humor.

She started by going to the cookie shop, and after she'd gorged herself with her favorite gooey chocolate-chip cookies that were still warm from the oven, she went into a lingerie shop, where the prices were outrageously high and the things that went into the bags she carried out were outra-

172

geously skimpy. Then she decided to treat herself to a skin analysis by a cosmetics expert who was having a one-day seminar at Macy's.

When the woman was done with her, Lauren looked into the mirror and nearly gasped out loud. She looked . . . exotic. Her eyebrows were darker than normal, but she had to admit that she liked the effect. Green and gray shadows accentuated the slant of her eyes, and a dark-green pencil had been used on her lower lid to intensify the color of her irises.

"I don't know," she said doubtfully, looking at her mouth. It seemed more generous, outlined in brown and glossed a deep crimson.

"It takes a little getting used to," she admitted. The color on her lips was gorgeous, if a bit bold. But she felt extravagant. "I'll take the lipstick."

With her purchases squeezed into one plastic bag, Lauren was walking through the parking lot, looking for her car, when a pleasant, very familiar male voice called her name.

She turned, smiling. "Rob!" She waited, and when he was nearly to her, she asked, "Is Jeanne cleaning you out again?"

He grinned, a flash of strong white teeth. "No. I'm alone. Jeanne's gone off with the kids to the ball game. And I decided, since they neglected to get a ticket for me, I would do a little shopping. You know, get ahead of the game for a change."

Curious to find out if the kids were "punishing" him for lowering the boom on Donnie, she asked, "How come they forgot to get you a ticket?"

"They figured I wouldn't be home in time to go with them, so they just didn't bother." A boyish smile spread over his face. "I was going to have dinner first. How about joining me? Unless, of course, you have to rush home?"

No, there was no reason to rush. There was no one waiting for her at home. "I'd love to. Just let me put these packages in my car," she said, happy to have a reason not to go to her big, empty house just yet.

"Here, let me take that for you." He took the bag, and as they were walking to her car, his hand warmly clasped her arm. "You're looking gorgeous," he whispered, giving her arm a gentle squeeze.

"Thank you." Oh, Lord! Lauren thought, emotion knotting in her throat. She felt so fragile that, if he was too sweet to her, she would very probably fall to pieces!

Rob seemed to sense her mood, and during dinner he went out of his way to cheer her. Politics were his passion, but his job as vice-president for a major bank was what supported his family. Anecdotes of his daily encounters with loan applicants were what had tears of laughter chasing each other down her cheeks.

"I'm glad to see you laughing again," he said mildly, reaching out to wipe a tear from the corner of her mouth. "Colby, huh?"

She understood what he meant, and nodded. "It's not working out." Her smile trembled. "He tells me that he loves me, but I don't know. Who the hell knows?" she muttered with feeling. "Maybe the problem's just with me. Maybe I'm just not right for him." A long sigh shuddered through her slim body. "I had such dreams. I guess I wanted too much." Misty eyed, she smiled up at him. "I guess what I wanted was what you and Jeanne have. You're so lucky—"

"It's not all luck, honey," Rob interrupted gently. "In fact, it's a helluva lot of work, to tell you the truth," he added with a quick, rather embarrassed laugh.

"I am—was—willing to work very hard to make a go of it, Rob. But Colby wasn't—isn't even trying." The emotions raging through her were an equal mixture of helplessness and frustration. Frustration because she felt she had tried very hard to be accommodating, understanding, and where had it got her? Helplessness because even now she wished with all her heart that she could turn back the clock and start all over again.

"Maybe he's afraid," Rob suggested, running the tip of one finger around the rim of his beer glass, while his eyes, filled with sympathy, remained fixed on her unhappy expression.

"Of what?"

"Of you. Of making that final Till-death-do-us-part commitment," he murmured.

"No, I don't think that's it." Colby wasn't afraid of anything, except possibly admitting that he was not as indispensable to the police force as he presumed himself to be, judging by his actions.

"Give him a chance, honey," Rob advised, winking at her. "He's a good man." He chuckled softly. "Even your father likes him."

"The barometer for all relationships, Matthew Shayler," she mocked, laughing with him. "I'll never forget the night that Jeanne said she was going to go to dinner with you. 'What does he want with you?' he shouted, and went on to tell her that you were too old for her, that it wasn't seemly for you to be seen with your children's baby-sitter, for goodness' sakes!"

Rob chortled. "That's nothing compared to what he's saying about Colby pursuing you, his 'baby.' "

Lauren didn't want to hear what her father, her family, thought of Colby, and would forever be grateful that they hadn't known that he and she had been living together. "I can well imagine," she said quietly.

Rob knew that tone, that shuttered look. He smiled. "Well, it looks like I've put it off long enough." He reached into his pocket for his wallet, took out a credit card, and then motioned the waitress over to ask for their check.

"What do you suggest I get for your sister's birthday?" he asked as they were walking out of the restaurant.

"Get her anything but cologne. The kids already bought her a gallon of it."

"How about a negligée?"

A mischievous smile dimpled Lauren's cheeks. "Why waste the money when she won't wear it long?"

"Ah, but then I'd miss the fun of taking it off her," he teased with a hoarse laugh.

She laughed with him, and as he was walking her to her car, Lauren felt happier and more relaxed than she had all day.

A shock awaited her when she got home. The door was unlocked, and for the space of a heartbeat Lauren mentally raged against Maggie for leaving her home vulnerable to intruders.

She lowered her bag quietly to the floor and had taken one careful step forward when Colby's voice demanded from the living room, "Where the hell have you been?"

Startled, Lauren snapped, "With Rob!"

"I see."

Something in his expression vexed her. "What is it you think you see, Colby?" she asked, somehow managing to keep her voice from cracking under the strain.

"That I shouldn't have bothered busting my fanny to get home to you."

Lauren didn't want to fight. She took a step toward him, smiling, struggling inwardly to maintain that smile when it wasn't returned. If there was any hope of salvaging their relationship, they needed to talk, to come to terms with their problems. And she wasn't too proud to make the first move.

"I'm sorry I wasn't here," she said. "But Tish canceled dinner because Mark couldn't be there, so I went shopping. I met Rob at the mall, and since we were both alone, we decided to have dinner together."

There was disbelief stamped on his features as he looked down his nose at her, and when he spoke his voice was tightly controlled. "Happy coincidence, wasn't it?"

Lauren shook her head. It was no use. She stepped back, took up her bag, and moved with it toward her bedroom, feeling vaguely tearful. Suddenly she felt very, very tired, and knew that if she stayed with him, she would dissolve in tears. And that would solve nothing.

Lauren took out some of her frustrations in biting off price tags and throwing her purchases willy-nilly into the appropriate drawers. When she heard Colby's strident footsteps heading her way, she stiffened, drew in a deep breath for control, and continued with what she was doing.

"I'm going out for a bite. I thought, maybe, you'd like to go along for the ride?"

Hope burgeoned in her heart, glowed in the eyes that looked up at him, sweetened the smile that played across her mouth. "Give me a sec to wash this gunk off my face, please?"

His gaze went over her slowly, appreciatively, before he whispered, "You look stunning."

"Thank you." She laughed. "In that case, let's go."

They didn't talk on the way to the all-night restaurant, but Lauren was just as happy to be silent. She studied him unobtrusively, noted that he looked tired, tense. Her gaze went slowly to the hands that were curled tightly around the wheel. The knuckles showed strain. They were strong hands, gentle hands. A smile flitted across her lips as she remembered how tender those hands could be, the warmth that radiated through her body each time those long, strong fingers caressed her intimately. With a longing that left her breathless, Lauren turned to look out the window.

While he was waiting for his dinner, he deftly maneuvered her into telling him all about her shopping spree, the time she had spent with Rob, what they had eaten, what they had talked about. Pretending mild curiosity, he pressed to know whether she and Rob had left together.

He was treating her like a suspect under interrogation. Lauren was tempted to tell him that she was well aware of what he was doing. But she decided against it. She had nothing to feel guilty about, and if knowing helped him with whatever was bothering him, she was happy to oblige him.

As he picked up their check, Colby seemed to be more relaxed. "It's early yet, so how about going for a ride?"

"Sounds marvelous." Lauren smiled happily, anticipating parking somewhere and in the privacy of the car's interior discussing their problems. She wasn't expecting that they would resolve them all in one fell swoop, but she was looking forward to getting them all out in the open and clearing the air between them.

When Colby headed north, Lauren assumed they were going up into the Berkeley Hills. She leaned back with a grateful smile. Despite the rain—or perhaps because of it—that had made the morning raw and gloomy, it was a beautiful night, with a sky that was clear and dotted with stars. The air was fresh, if a little crisp.

Why am I surprised? she wondered miserably as Colby brought the car to a stop some ten minutes later. She didn't have to look through the windshield to know where they were. She drew a deep breath, wishing he had taken them somewhere else—*anywhere* but here.

"What's wrong now?"

Whether it was the abruptness of his question or the sight of the police station that nettled her more, Lauren couldn't tell, but whichever it was, it was the last straw. "Why should there be anything wrong?" Her voice was shaky with irritation, her hands were trembling so badly she had to clench them on her lap. "I mean, where else would you go on such a beautiful night but to the police station?"

Colby hesitated for a moment, then turned fully toward her, the light from the streetlamps catching the gold highlights in his hair and accentuating the harsh lines that bracketed his mouth. He stared at her steadily as he rested his knee on the console and his arm on the back of his seat.

"I thought, maybe, if you could see where I work, you

178

would be able to cope with your jealousy, stop thinking of my work as your rival." The words were clipped, the tone impatient.

She swallowed hard, then forced her eyes up to meet his unwavering stare. "You don't understand, do you?" she said quietly. "It's not the place, or the job, Colby. It's you." She inhaled sharply. "Or maybe it's me. I don't think I know anymore."

"It's not you." He laughed, but it was not a pleasant sound. "It's me." He drew in a slow, steadying breath, making a real effort to choke off the anger that was swelling his breast before it could choke him. "I'm not an eight-to-five office jock, and even for you—"

"I never asked you to—"

"I love you, Lauren, but I can't treat you like 'the icing on the cake,'" he said with a cynical twist of his mouth. "Personally I prefer the cake to the frosting." His eyes, as they focused on her crimson lips, were cold and angry.

Lauren chose not to dignify his icing-on-the-cake remark. Rob had meant something entirely different from the connotation Colby in his anger was putting on the compliment.

"And I won't be 'on call' for you or anyone else."

In an abrupt, irritated movement, Colby straightened and turned the ignition key, starting the car. Wheels squealing, he tore down the street, and violated all the traffic laws he worked so hard to uphold in his haste to get her home.

He parked the car on her driveway, and as he started to leave it to go help her out, she said, "Don't bother," and turned to open her own door; but he stopped her.

"I love you, Lauren," he said, his hand relaxing its grip on her wrist.

"I believe you do, in your own fashion. But that's not good enough, Colby." Her face was blanched as she looked him right in the eyes, her own eyes overbright with tears. "I want someone who's not afraid to give all of himself, just like I'm not afraid to give you all of me."

"What's left after you give so much to everyone else," he grated, taking out his frustrations on the door, viciously flinging it outward.

"What's that supposed to mean?"

"That after you have expended all your energies on re-arranging Tish's love life, or counseling Jeanne on how to raise her children, or bullying your parents into taking a vacation they don't want, or being the councilman's sounding board, there's nothing left for me, or for any man."

He might as well have slapped her. The effect was the same. Looking like a child unjustly accused of cheating on an exam, Lauren bolted from the car, a sob choking her breath.

She had only taken a few steps when she heard the car door slamming shut. And then, tires squealing, Colby backed out of her driveway and raced down the street as though he were answering a call for help. Lauren opened the door and rushed into the house, flinging herself onto the couch with a pained cry.

In the days that followed, Lauren kept herself too busy to think, to remember, to regret. Without her work she might not have been able to endure the pain and heartbreak.

She saw Colby once while she was at the post office, but he turned away, pretending not to see her. It was then that she knew, with a chilling certainty, that she had joined the ranks of former lovers.

Two long, torturous weeks after the night she'd ended it with Colby, Lauren finally came to terms with her emotions. Not that she was happy, or even content. Resigned. That was the word. The pain of missing him had lessened to a dull ache, and she pretended, even to herself, that she was on the mend.

She fooled no one.

Especially not her grandmother, who had never approved of her slimness to begin with.

It was Saturday and Lauren had taken her grandmother to the mall to shop for a gift for an old friend. They shopped for a few hours, and Lauren fought hard not to show any impatience as they walked from one end of the mall to the other, her grandmother showing a total lack of interest in everything the shops had to offer. Finally, at one o'clock, Lauren suggested they have lunch.

"It's about time," Catherine remarked. "And I want to see you order something substantial," she added, her tone implying she would not tolerate having her order salad and soup, which was all her stomach could stand lately. In her inimitable way Catherine pointed out that she looked so bad, it was a wonder someone hadn't mistaken her for a manne-quin.

"Thank you, Gram. I knew I could count on you to cheer me up," Lauren mocked, but she understood why her grand-mother was so concerned. She had lost weight, and there was a hollow look surrounding her eyes that accentuated the gauntness of her cheeks. Cosmetics didn't help.

That other time, when she had walked out on Johnny Tolan, the warm, loving support of her family was what had kept her from coming completely unhinged. Lauren knew that between them and her work, she had a strong chance for surviving this devastating blow.

"Tell you what, you old nag," she said, injecting, for the sake of her grandmother's peace of mind, a familiar teasing quality into her voice. "How about if you come stay with me for a while, and make me some of those wonderfully fatten-ing meals you're famous for?" She put an arm around Catherine's shoulders and gave her a loving hug.

"Thank you, dear. Your father's been raging around the house like a wounded bear about something or other, and it would be nice to get away from him for a while." She patted Lauren's arm. "I prefer your company anyway."

Lauren quickly looked away as sudden tears blurred her

vision, and she tried frantically to blink them away before her grandmother noticed.

"Come on now, don't dawdle," instructed Catherine, taking hold of Lauren's arm and pulling her toward the Marble Club. "When we went past here, I noticed the special was sole *almondine.*"

Which meant she was going to have the special whether or not she wanted it, Lauren thought. But she gave in with good grace, knowing her grandmother was bullying her only because she was concerned for her.

"Ouch! Damn!" Colby lowered his hand and, for the space of a heartbeat, stared at the blood that was oozing from a small cut on his chin and flowing down to dampen the collar of his pajama top.

He'd had a hellish night. One of many. Lauren's memory was merciless, strong, determined. Even when he succeeded in sleeping, her image floated in and out of his dreams.

"You're a damned fool," he told the hollow-eyed reflection in the mirror.

And unlike Lauren, he couldn't lose himself in his work.

A hard, mocking laugh erupted from his mouth, bouncing off the walls, returning to taunt him.

How she would laugh if she only knew that the job he had thought so important had lost its appeal. He realized now that she'd been right all along. He had been so obsessed with his job he had made her feel unimportant. And no woman liked to be taken for granted. It was a wonder Lauren had put up with it for as long as she had. He flung down his razor with a muttered curse.

Turning on his heel, totally unmindful of the wound on his chin, of the blood staining his top, he strode across the tiled floor, stomping over clothes that littered his bedroom floor in his hurry to get to the phone.

He was going to call her to ask her forgiveness. He had to make her see that she was what mattered most in his life.

His job was important to him, it would always be, but it would never again be the dominating force in his life. And if he hadn't lost Lauren forever, if she would give him a second chance, he would prove to her that he could change. With her help he would develop a healthier work schedule.

But what if she no longer wants you?

The hand holding the phone trembled slightly.

He had to take a chance. He wanted her, needed her. Without her his life had no zest. Resolutely, he dialed her number, and while he was waiting for her to answer, an idea came to him. It was silly, risky—

"Hello?"

His voice was so choked it was barely audible when he whispered, "I have it on good authority you're looking for a full-time lover." He paused, waiting for Lauren to say something, and when she didn't, he went on, his voice a low husky drawl. "I'd like to apply for the job." When his suggestion was met with silence, he plunged both feet into it. "I come with very good references. If you would grant me a private interview I will show you what an excellent lover I can be. I will take you on a roller-coaster ride of passion, I will make love to you in the kitchen, the living room, and the hallway. I will love you until you plead for mercy and then I'll . . ."

He inhaled sharply when he heard Catherine's voice, shaky with suppressed laughter, saying, "Laurie, honey, I think it's for you."

"Oh, Lord, I didn't know it was you!" he exclaimed, feeling like a chump for following what, at best, had been the crazy impulse of a man who didn't know what to do to get back in his woman's good graces.

"Another wrong number, Lieutenant?"

"Lauren?"

"Yes."

"Now that I've made a total idiot of myself, I may as well go all the way. I want to come see you."

Lauren said nothing.

"Please?"

"Can the city spare you?"

"Ouch," he murmured good-naturedly. "Look, I really want to come see you. We need to talk."

"All right."

"I'll be there in five minutes."

Lauren answered his first knock. Something about her posture and the solemn look in her eyes made him very uncomfortable.

"May I come in?"

"Please do." Her voice was cool, withdrawn.

He followed her into the living room and saw that Catherine was lounging on the sofa.

"Hello, Colby," she said pleasantly.

"Hello," he said, smiling, glad that at least one member of the Shayler clan was still speaking to him. The rest, whom he'd run into at one time or another during the past couple of weeks, had treated him as if he were a leper.

"You youngsters don't need me," Catherine announced, dropping her feet to the floor, searching for and finding her blue scuffs. Gathering her glasses and the book she had been reading, she said good-night and slipped out of the room.

"You win," he said simply.

"Oh? We were in some competition I didn't know about?" She was standing very straight, almost stiff, and her eyes were shuttered, concealing whatever thoughts were running through her mind.

"You're not going to make it easy for me, are you?" he asked.

She shook her head.

"I'm a proud, stubborn man, Lauren." He looked at her, his eyes begging her to help him, but she remained mulishly silent. "It's never been easy for me to apologize, to beg for anything, but I'm begging you now, Laurie. Give me, us,

184

another chance. I give you my word that I'll do everything in my power to make it a good life for both of us."

A muscle pulsed uncontrollably at her jawline. "Give me one good reason why I should trust you and give you another chance to hurt me."

He winced. "Like I said before, you really go for the jugular, don't you?"

She lifted her chin a fraction. "And I told you before, I won't be 'on call' for any man."

"I don't want you to be. I know that's how I made you feel, but it wasn't what I wanted. I fell for you so damned hard that it rattled me, shook my self-confidence, and I didn't like it. So I went out of my way, unconsciously, to assert myself with you, to both our sorrow. I resented the time you devoted to your family, and instead of admitting that I was jealous I used that as an excuse to justify spending all my time at work.

"Forgive me, Laurie, for taking you for granted and abusing the love you gave so freely."

He made a move toward her, and when she didn't bolt, closed the inches that separated them. "I realize now that there are other things besides my job that are important in my life. You, for instance." His arms surrounded her, holding her lightly, afraid that if he followed his heart's desire, he would crush her, hurt her. "I'm not ever going to hurt you, honey," he promised. "I love you too much."

"I love you too," she whispered. "But I want time, Colby."

He hadn't anticipated this, but he was willing to take her on whatever terms she dictated, at least until she learned to trust him again.

"How much time, sweetheart?"

"As long as it takes for you to learn to give all of yourself without fear."

He smiled against her hair. "I'll spend the rest of my life

proving to you that I'm no longer afraid—that loving you is the only thing important in my life."

Lauren lifted her radiant face to his, her eyes misty with happiness. She smiled as his mouth moved downward, and opened her lips to invite his exploration of her mouth. She knew he couldn't change overnight, but she was happy just knowing that he was willing to try.

And they were together, which was all that really mattered.

JAYNE CASTLE

excites and delights you with
tales of adventure and romance

____ TRADING SECRETS

Sabrina had wanted only a casual vacation fling with the rugged Matt. But the extraordinary pull between them made that impossible. So did her growing relationship with his son—and her daring attempt to save the boy's life.
19053-3-15 $3.50

____ DOUBLE DEALING

Jayne Castle sweeps you into the corporate world of multimillion dollar real estate schemes and the very private world of executive lovers. Mixing business with pleasure, they made *passion* their bottom line.
12121-3-18 $3.95

Come Faith, Come Fire

Vanessa Royall

Proud as her aristocratic upbringing, bold as the
ancient gypsy blood that ran in her veins, the
beautiful golden-haired Maria saw her family burned
at the stake and watched her young love, forced into
the priesthood. Desperate and bound by a forbidden
love, Maria defies the Grand Inquisitor himself and
flees across Spain to a burning love that was destined
to be free! $2.95

All-new
Candlelight Newsletter

**An exceptional,
free offer awaits readers
of Dell's incomparable Candlelight Ecstasy and Supreme Romances.**

Subscribe to our all-new CANDLELIGHT NEWSLETTER
and you will receive—at absolutely no cost to you—exciting, ex-
clusive information about today's finest romance novels and nov-
elists. You'll be part of a select group to receive sneak previews of
upcoming Candlelight Romances, well in advance of publication.

You'll also go behind the scenes to "meet" our Ecstasy
and Supreme authors, learning firsthand where they get their
ideas and how they made it to the top. News of author appear-
ances and events will be detailed, as well. And contributions from
the Candlelight editor will give you the inside scoop on how she
makes her decisions about what to publish—and how *you* can try
your hand at writing an Ecstasy or Supreme.

You'll find all this and more in Dell's CANDLELIGHT
NEWSLETTER. And best of all, *it costs you nothing*. That's right!
It's Dell's way of thanking our loyal Candlelight readers and of
adding another dimension to your reading enjoyment.

Just fill out the coupon below, return it to us, and look forward to receiving the first of many CANDLELIGHT NEWS-
LETTERS—overflowing with the kind of excitement that only
enhances our romances!